Also by Mavis Jukes

Like Jake and Me
Blackberries in the Dark
It's a Girl Thing: How to Stay Healthy, Safe, and in Charge
Growing Up: It's a Girl Thing
Expecting the Unexpected
Planning the Impossible
Cinderella 2000
The Guy Book: An Owner's Manual
You're a Bear
Be Healthy! It's a Girl Thing: Food, Fitness, and Feeling Great

SM⬤KE

MAVIS JUKES

A NOVEL

SM⦿KE

Farrar, Straus and Giroux
New York

Copyright © 2009 by Mavis Jukes
All rights reserved
Distributed in Canada by Douglas & McIntyre Ltd.
Printed in the United States of America
Designed by Jonathan Bartlett
First edition, 2009
10 9 8 7 6 5 4 3 2 1

www.fsgkidsbooks.com

Library of Congress Cataloging-in-Publicaton Data
Jukes, Mavis.
    Smoke / Mavis Jukes.— 1st ed.
        p.   cm.
    Summary: Twelve-year-old Colton and his mother move to a farm in California,
away from his grandfather and his rodeo-champion father in Idaho, and after his cat
Smoke goes missing, Colt feels even more lonely for his old life.
    ISBN-13: 978-0-374-37085-5
    ISBN-10: 0-374-37085-0
    [1. Single-parent families—Fiction.   2. Change—Fiction.   3. Cats—Fiction.
4. Lost and found possessions—Fiction.   5. Country life—California—Fiction.
6. California—Fiction.]   I. Title.

PZ7.J9294Sm 2009
[Fic]—dc22

                                                                            2008007157

For Bob Hink and Jane Sterzinger

Thanks to Frances Foster
Also thanks to: Bill Allan, Sharon Arnold, Jaimi Baer,
Ruth Barron, Matt Boyd, Pat Dahl, Teri Glazier, Roger Hollander,
Bob Hudson, Jim Jard, Amy Jukes-Hudson, River Jukes-Hudson,
Louise Lash, Milly Lee, Jonah Raskin, George Viramontes,
and Allan Yeager

Special thanks to:
Dino Ruffoni, Hidden Valley School counselor

SM⬤KE

One

Colton, his mom, and his dad were sitting in the Wagon Wheel cafe in a booth with maroon upholstery, next to the window. Colton poured a little salt on the table and drove his finger around in it.

"You listening, Colt?"

"Yup."

His dad crumpled up his paper napkin. "So right after Christmas, you come on back to Idaho for a few days. Visit with Grandpa. He's going to be alone."

"What about you, Dad?"

"Uncle Chad's on leave then. Him and me are going fishing in Baja. But end of July, it's gonna be you, me, Grandpa, and Uncle Chad on the ranch. The barn needs a new roof."

"Okay."

"Afternoons we'll ride out to the South Fork. Got to see if one of us can break your record for that six-pound brown you got last year."

Colton smiled a little, remembering the look on his dad's face when he landed that trout on the riverbank. "Yeah, well, you can try anyway."

Colton's mom frowned. "Jesse? Sugar rule."

"Yes, ma'am."

"I mean it, Jesse. That's the one and only horse I want him on, and nothing's going to change about that."

"I said Yes, ma'am."

"And I don't want Colton up on that roof! If you and your brother want to take a nosedive off the roof, that's up to you, but I'd like to get Colton back in one piece if that's okay."

"Yes, ma'am." A black Ford roadster pulled into the parking lot. "Check it out, Colt. It's a '32." Colton and his dad stared out the window.

"And, Jesse?" said his mom. "Like I told you, the game plan is for Colt and me to try California out for a year or two, but it could be longer. Frank says stay as long as we want."

"I heard you the first time, Celeste. We've been through this. Haven't we? Well, just tell that old great-uncle Frank of yours hi from me and thanks for that note he sent me a few years back. You want that last piece of bacon?"

"No, have it. What note?"

Colton's dad stuck the bacon in his mouth and stood up.

"Celeste?" He finished his last swallow of coffee and wiped his mouth on the back of his hand. "You don't want to know." He took his white straw Stetson off a hook on the wall. "We'll go over the details with the mediator. Okay, darlin'? It'll all be official." He put on his hat and set it toward the back of his head. "I'm comin' through again in a couple of weeks."

"Where you headed now?"

"Jackson."

He slid his thumbs behind his big gold and silver belt buckle and hitched up his jeans. He was wearing new boots.

"J. B. Hills?" Celeste asked.

"Yeah." Jesse pulled up a pant leg and showed her his boot top: mahogany leather, piped with white, and one big white star on the front. "Got 'em in Cody."

"Nice."

"Thanks." He dug into the pocket of his Wranglers and left a twenty-dollar bill on the table. "I'm one phone call away and don't forget it," he told Colton.

"I won't." Colton put on his hat. "Do you e-mail, Dad?"

"Me?"

"Just thought I'd ask."

"Okay then. Take care, Colt."

"I will."

They bumped fists.

"You too, Celeste."

"Right. Don't forget your sunglasses."

Outside, Colton and his dad looked into the roadster.

"Just remember, Colt. Big windshield, little rearview mirror."

Whatever that meant.

They didn't say goodbye. They never did.

Colton's dad tipped his hat to Celeste.

She called, "Bye, Jess. Thanks for breakfast. Take care now."

He got into his pickup and drove out of the parking lot, with country music blasting.

Colton wondered when he'd see him again. Just like he had every time his dad drove away, ever since he could remember.

Colton and his mom got into an old Volvo station wagon. "Well, judging from the boots, he must be doing okay for himself," his mom said quietly. She fished around for her keys.

She started the car. "You okay with all this?" she asked.

"Yeah, sure."

"You know I didn't make this decision lightly."

"Yeah, I know, Mom. Don't worry about it."

And Colton really didn't want his mom to worry about it. Even a kid could see she was in a rut. She'd been a hostess and a bookkeeper at the same steak house in Idaho Falls since Colton was two—ten years.

It was definitely time for her to move on.

But was Colton okay with all of this?

Leave his friends? How could he be okay with that?

Colton had been born and raised in big sky country; it was home, and always would be.

Leave his grandpa? Who knew how long he'd be around?

Moving out to California would take Colton farther away from his dad and he'd see him less. But it wasn't like he saw him all that often to begin with. His dad had come in and out of Colton's life, mainly out. Not because he didn't care but because he was on the rodeo circuit, which kept him on the road most of the time.

But it wasn't only the rodeo. What made it harder for Colton and his dad to spend time together was that his mom couldn't have been more disapproving of his dad's lifestyle; so no rodeo weekends, even when the rodeo was close by. He saw his dad two or three times a year, holidays sometimes. And for a few days every summer at his grandpa's ranch.

He hoped the move would be temporary.

Not that he didn't want his mom to succeed. But imagining his mom as a farmer was a stretch. Her great-uncle Frank had talked her into coming out to California to live rent-free in his country place. He said the house was lonely, that it wanted a family in it. He had a Ford pickup to lend to Celeste, a neighbor to help out, and plenty of fertile land for her to try organic farming. All she needed were seeds and a business plan. He'd help with that. She already had a green thumb.

Frank said if she made a go of the business, she could stay

forever, for all he cared. He didn't have any kids or grand-kids, and Celeste was the only one of his four grandnieces and grandnephews who ever paid attention to him, except to call him on holidays.

Celeste had stayed with him and Taylor way back when, when she tried culinary school in San Francisco. When she was just out of high school.

Frank and Taylor owned a high-rise apartment. They lived in the penthouse—with a Picasso in the bathroom.

If anybody knew how to make a business plan, it was Frank.

Celeste discussed the move with her friends and Colton's teachers. She took Colton's feelings into account, not that he told her the truth. She sublet their house on Pine Street in Idaho Falls. The owner of the steak house, Diane, sat and cried. "I'm going to miss you so much, Celeste. Colton, too." She said she'd welcome Colton's mom back, anytime. And give Colton a job busing dishes, when he was older. If he wanted.

Colton and his mom went through everything, then had a yard sale. Colton kept his piggy bank with the silly grin; that was from his grandpa, and he kept his savings in it. But he put out his picture books, toys, Batman Halloween cos-tume, too-small clothes, too-small boots, and too-small baseball mitts. He was sad to see his plastic action figures lying in the grass, but at twelve he figured it was time to leave his toys behind.

Yeah, it was sad. But he took it like a man.

Colton's mom gave away most of her beautiful house-plants. They put the sagging corduroy couch and matching easy chair on the lawn with a sign on each that said "Free."

Smoke, Colton's twenty-pound, jet-black Maine coon cat, stretched out on the couch like a jaguar.

Will and Brady, Colton's best friends, and their parents threw a surprise goodbye party at the park—a big barbecue, with ribs, ranch beans, corn on the cob, potato salad, and a sheet cake with "Good Luck" written on it. Everybody was there. Well, not everybody. His dad was on a roundup somewhere. But his baseball coaches came and so did Diane from the steak house, kids from his class and his baseball team, and even his teacher, Mrs. Barron.

The grownups played horseshoes and volleyball, kids played baseball. It was hard to be there—hard not to let his feelings show.

Colton asked to spend his last couple of days in Idaho with his grandpa—at the ranch, two and a half hours away. They set out on Saturday, early.

Colton's mom was wary of the situation at the ranch and had tolerated it for years—but only with plenty of rules in place. Rule Number One: No shooting.

Colton could live with that. Not that he judged his dad, uncle, or grandpa for hunting. Sure, he liked venison jerky and elk steaks, and venison stew. But as for himself, he def-initely would go with shooting pictures over shooting ani-mals. He liked drawing pictures, too. And he was good at it. In fact, great at it.

Who knew where that talent came from in the gene pool—maybe from Frank. He was a designer. Definitely not from Colton's mom or dad.

His dad couldn't draw his way out of a paper bag.

His mom was worse.

Colton turned and asked her: "Did you pack the Pictionary game?"

"Of course."

"That's what I was afraid of."

His mom couldn't draw a stick figure, and playing Pictionary with her as his teammate was a guaranteed loss. "Well, if we play in California, I'll be on Frank's team."

"What an insult."

"Remember that shoe you drew last time we played that looked like a frying pan?"

"No it did not."

"The heel looked like a handle."

"It was a high-heeled shoe."

Colton looked out the car window. He saw a couple of Appaloosas nuzzling each other. Horses: another sore subject and the source of Rule Number Two.

Colton's grandpa had broken his hip in a horse wreck when he was a young man. Colton's dad had broken his back at the rodeo in Jackson Hole, just after Colton was born. Likewise, Colton's uncle Chad had broken bones—too many to count.

So Rule Number Two: Colton rode only Sugar, his grandpa's calm, wide old mare.

Sure, his mother was overprotective in regard to the horses, anybody could see that. But Colton was afraid if he protested too much, he wouldn't get to go to the ranch at all.

Anyway, he loved to ride Sugar. Who wouldn't—sweet as she was, out in open country, with the smell of sage so thick in the air. And Sugar wasn't always slow. Not that Colton would have reported that to his mom.

Colton loved everything he knew about ranching. As for the rodeo, Colton was on the line about that.

His mom saw the rodeo as entertainment—at the expense of calves, horses, cattle. Sometimes they got hurt, too. She didn't see the point of throwing down calves and tying them up, scaring them half to death.

Colton didn't necessarily agree with his mom on that. And he definitely did look up to the rodeo cowboys, and the cowgirls. Competing in what they did best—and needed to do on a cattle ranch. Roping and riding. All that.

Bull riding didn't serve much purpose, though—not for ranching anyway.

One thing for sure: it kept his dad on the road.

For the past few years, he had been going to Paris with his girlfriend, Cheryl, to be in the Wild West Show. Cheryl was a trick rider, a champion. She said sometime they'd take Colton, but Colton wasn't holding his breath waiting for that to happen.

He liked Cheryl; she was nice. But Colton decided not to give his dad, Cheryl, the rodeo, or Paris much more thought as he and his mom followed the white line down the highway. They slowed and turned at the little old dented mailbox with HUDSON painted on it. They bumped along the two ruts toward the cottonwoods, past the old shed that had gone down, roof on the ground and grass growing through. His grandpa Wes was walking down the driveway to meet them. His limp had gotten worse. He needed a cane, but he was too proud to use one.

Grandpa was always happy to see Colton and Celeste. They visited awhile on the porch, drank iced tea, and ate Nilla wafers out of a box. "So what all does it take to get you a good crop of lettuce going?" Grandpa asked, and Celeste smiled.

"Well, I don't know, Wes, to be honest. Guess I'll find out."

"And this Frank, will he be around to help you?"

"He has a neighbor in the country who's been looking after the place for a few years, so he's lined up to help me."

"Well, that's good. And you got Colt, too. And he's growing like a weed. How tall are you now, boy?"

"He's five seven," Celeste said.

"Already?" Colton's grandpa bopped him on the shoulder. "You'll be built so high up your feet won't reach the ground. You two driving the Volvo out?"

"No. My friend's buying it from me. We got a rental truck. Frank has a loaner pickup for us when we get there."

"A Ford," Colton added. "Four-by-four."

"Well, that's good."

Colton's mom and Grandpa made some small talk and then said their goodbyes. It was a long ride home, so Celeste didn't linger.

Colton and his grandpa watched her get to the end of the road. When she turned onto the highway, Grandpa said, "Well, what are we waitin' for?"

The sunlight was yellow in the treetops. The air was clean and cool. Colton and his grandpa saddled up and rode out to their favorite spot on the river for fishing—and poking around. Yeah, Colton liked Sugar okay; she was a good old girl. And pretty, too, with her pale yellow mane and tail. Colton rested his face against her cheek and patted her neck after he tied her up to a tree branch in the meadow near the riverbank. She whinnied softly, from deep in her throat.

They put together the fishing rods. But it was too windy to cast, even roll cast. The trout weren't hungry, but Colton was. His grandpa had a plastic package of hot dogs in his saddlebag; he took the package out and stuck it into his jacket pocket before they crossed the river.

Colton was right behind him, ready to grab the back of his jacket. His grandpa almost went down, but he caught himself before Colton did. Colton pretended not to see. But he wondered just how many more trips his grandpa would be able to make across that cold, fast-moving water, with the loose rocks. Not many. And that was a sad thought. So he decided not to think it anymore.

His grandpa put a rock on top of the hot dog package to keep the dogs cool in the water.

Just like always, they explored the old cabin site, with only the chimney standing. Brush was growing through the floor. Every time they went, they found something good. Colton's grandpa picked up an old, shot-up Wyoming license plate and gave it to Colton as a souvenir. He said to Colton, "I'm hungry, are you?"

The Hudson boys were always hungry.

They made a circle of flat river rocks, gathered up some dry sage, twigs, and small sticks, and built a fire on the sandbar, close to the water. Colton lit it, with his grandpa supervising and approving. They cooked the dogs over the fire, speared on green willow branches stripped of their leaves.

They sat and said nothing—just chewing and listening to the river. Colton watched the smoke rise up against the blue sky. A butterfly fluttered and landed on a rock near the water. And Colton's grandpa told him: "Now that's the closest thing to proof I ever had of heaven.

"A caterpillar spins itself a cocoon. Next thing you know it wakes up and flies away."

Colton watched the butterfly open and close its wings.

"Okay, Colt," said Grandpa. "I guess we better git."

Colton carried water in a leaky, half-squashed bucket to douse the fire. They watched it steam, heard it hiss. Colton stirred the wet ashes with a stick and then he added more water to make sure the fire was out. His grandpa had taught him all about fire: how to build one with just one match, when and where and how to burn one, and when not to, and how to put one out. Colton's grandpa was a regular old Smokey Bear when it came to campfires and fires in the woodstove. Back when he was a kid, a chimney fire had burnt his family's ranch house down, and everyone had been lucky to get out alive. He'd told the story several times to Colton, but Colton never got tired of his grandpa's stories. In fact, later he might ask Grandpa to tell him that chimney story again.

Colton looked down at the fire ring in the sand and the wet, shining, blackened charcoal sticks floating inside. He wondered how many more fires there would be on the riverbank with his grandpa.

They crossed back over the river, same as before, with Colton behind, ready to catch his grandpa. The horses were restless, like they always were when something was around. "Maybe a bear," his grandpa noted. "Or a moose." Colton wasn't scared of bears; there weren't any grizzlies. But he knew to watch his step with a mama moose, especially if she had a calf.

They headed back, up the rocky trail, with the landscape framed between Sugar's ears.

At home, they opened a couple of big cans of chunky beef stew and ate it cold right out of the cans along with a loaf of sheepherder's bread.

They sat at a picnic table in the middle of the meadow. "It's a cathedral." That's what his grandpa said when they watched the sun slip behind the mountains and light the clouds on fire.

When the sky turned deep blue, "There's Venus," his grandpa told Colton. "Last one out in the morning and first one out in the evening. I've hung a lot of wishes on that lucky star."

Later, they sat on the porch in metal chairs while the moon rolled into the sky. Colton's grandpa played his harmonica for a little while, made it sound like a train.

They watched the stars shoot and fall. Listened to the owls hoot.

"Out here on a rock, tumbling through space," his grandpa said. "Where an egg can turn into an owl. It's a miracle—at least that's how I see it."

They sat awhile without talking, just looking out at the night.

His grandpa had a little snort of whiskey—just one shot, for medicinal purposes. Then he said to Colton, "California —that's a long way from home."

"I know."

"But just remember, Colt, the same moon rises there as here. Look up, and that's a connection. I'll be lookin', too."

"Okay, Grandpa."

"Don't forget that."

"I won't."

Later, Colton asked his grandpa to tell the story about the horse with the ghost rider. Colton knew it by heart. He didn't believe in ghosts. But he almost did when he listened to his grandpa tell about the ghost rider, about the black horse's thundering hooves, its flared nostrils, its wild eyes with whites showing, its long black mane blowing back.

He pictured the empty saddle with silver trim, bright in the moonlight—and the empty fringed leather glove that loosely held the reins. He could see the empty boots—with skull and crossbones inlays, and silver spurs that drove the black horse on. Colton wasn't afraid of the ghost rider—he liked him. He wished he was real. He resolved to practice the ghost rider story and scare his mom silly with it the first stormy night in California.

Colton and his grandpa split a package of Oreo cookies, and finished off the milk for a late-night snack, then packed it in for the night. Colton slept on the couch.

On Sunday, goodbye was too hard to say. So Grandpa said, "See you, boy."

And Colton said, "Yeah."

Two

Colton and Celeste began the three-day drive from Idaho to California at dawn, in a sixteen-foot rental truck with a lift gate. They chose the truck with the bench seat—so there would be room in the cab for the cat carrier.

Most of the time, Colton let Smoke stand on his lap with his paws on the dash and look out the window. The cab was right over the engine; the engine was loud, and the seat was hard. It was like sitting on a board on top of a rock grinder.

Once they left Idaho Falls, the highway rolled out like a ribbon—nothing around but fences, sage, cattle, and sky. And cottonwoods, wherever there was water. They drove a few hours without talking much. Colton was mad about leaving, but he didn't let on; he just looked out the windshield. The Hudson boys didn't complain.

He kept his eye out for wildlife and saw quite a few ravens, a couple of hawks, and two huge birds with giant wingspans. He knew by the way they flapped their wings and soared that they were eagles; his grandpa had taught him that. Behind a billboard, Colton saw two bulls kicking up dust. So of course he thought of his dad.

The billboard said it was 68 miles to Jackpot. Colton was getting better at reading signs as they passed them, as long as the writing wasn't too much or too small. And as long as the truck wasn't going too fast, which it couldn't.

Colton and Celeste had been playing word games to help him with his reading. Lately, it was paying off.

"Let's play the game where we think of everything that's got the same word in it," he suggested to help pass the time.

"Okay, the word is . . . jack! Jackpot!" yelled Celeste.

"You're a cheater, Mom."

"I am not."

"I saw that sign, too."

"So what? Your turn."

Colton thought a minute. "Jackknife."

She said: "Jackrabbit."

He said: "Jackhammer."

She said: "Bootjack."

He said: "Carjack. Pull over, Mom. I'm driving from here on out."

They stopped to stretch at an abandoned gas station. The last three letters of the Standard sign had fallen off, so only the STAND was left standing. An old cinder-block building, with "Automotive Repair" painted on the side, was boarded closed. Broken glass sparkled and twinkled on the ground; the high desert stretched out beyond it.

Colton wrestled Smoke into the cat harness they'd bought at the Pet Stop and snapped a leash on the ring.

Humiliating, but too bad. The worst thing Colton could imagine would be losing Smoke out in the middle of nowhere. Or anywhere else, for that matter.

They got out and poked around. After a while Smoke got to business digging up a storm in the sand; Colton kept his eye out for snakes.

He picked up a rusty tobacco can and hung it from the rearview mirror with a piece of fence wire. "You're a worse pack rat than your grandpa," Celeste told him, which Colton considered a compliment.

The can tipped and squeaked on the wire as they headed on down the highway.

"What's the driving age in California anyway?" Colton asked.

"Eighteen, I think."

"It is?"

"Yup. And by the time you're eighteen, I hope it's twenty-one."

"Thanks, Mom."

"And I'm going to get you a car that doesn't go over fifty-five miles an hour. And that's downhill."

"Thanks, Mom."

For a while, the highway followed the train tracks. A Union Pacific freight car raced and clattered alongside them. Colton read out loud: "We promise to deliver."

They drove till the sun was low over the distant sandy hills. Then they stopped for the night at a truck stop that advertised diesel, propane, shrimp: all you can eat, for $6.95. "No thanks," Celeste mumbled. But pets were allowed and the parking lot was well lit.

They let Smoke prowl around the edge of the lot in the harness, brought in a disposable litter box, hauled in the cooler, made sandwiches, watched TV, and fell asleep—each in a queen-size bed. Smoke hogged Colton's bed, like he always did. By morning, Colton was just barely hanging on to one edge of the mattress.

He woke up to the sound of a big-nosed Kenworth warming up just outside the room. He peered through the blinds at the chrome bumper and yellow running lights.

They had cereal in Styrofoam bowls and juice in Styrofoam cups in the complimentary breakfast nook and were on the road before the sun came up. Colton could see Venus, sparkling on the horizon. It did look like a lucky star: one white spark over the desert in a sky turning turquoise blue. He made a wish: that his grandpa's hip would hold up okay.

The second day's drive was similar to the first: fences, sage, cattle, and sky. But they traveled on longer because the plan was to make it all the way to Reno.

The sunset looked like smoke and flames as the sun fell behind gray clouds and faraway, hazy purple hills.

Celeste said she knew of a casino with spacious, inexpensive rooms and a pool: the Golden Bounty Casino in Reno. As soon as they got into cell phone range, she called and made the reservation. The lonesome highway turned into a four-lane freeway, with more cars than they'd seen since Idaho Falls, all put together. Lights glimmered on the horizon. They took the downtown exit. A huge neon arrow pointed the way into the Golden Bounty.

Celeste said, "Okay, I admit it. This is the place I worked, back in the day."

"You got to be kidding me, Mom."

"Nope, I'm not. I was working here as a blackjack dealer the night I met your dad. He came into town for the rodeo. You know this."

Colton did, but he liked hearing it again.

"And there was a country band playing here. So he came in with his friends and had a few drinks. He sat down across from me: love at first sight. The rest is history."

"Was he any good at blackjack?"

"No. I took all his money."

Smoke stayed locked in the cab of the truck with the windows cracked, inside the Pet Taxi with a litter pan, food, and water. No worries; the night was cool. There was security in the lot. Colton's mom gave her credit card to a woman in a suit behind a long counter while slot machines rang behind them.

Near the concierge desk, Colton saw some Reno Rodeo posters in gold frames, and one posted for the season coming up.

His dad might be in the national finals. Maybe they could come back up to Reno to see him ride!

Sure, Colton told himself. Fat chance of that.

They put their suitcases in their room: tenth floor, nice digs. Great view of the mountains. Colton was starved as always, so they headed down to the Sea Foam restaurant.

"Culture shock," said Celeste as they hurried past people smoking cigarettes and playing slot machines and video poker. She waved her hand in front of her nose. "I can't believe I used to spend twelve hours a day here. See her?" She pointed to a pretty young woman dealing cards at a table. "That was me.

"To be honest, it was kind of fun," she added. "For a while, anyway."

There were mirrors everywhere in the Sea Foam, reflecting golden squid chandeliers with plastic streamers. Huge gray plastic sharks hung from the ceiling.

They both ordered fish and chips. Colton saved a piece of his fish for Smoke, wrapped it up in a napkin and snuck it into his mom's purse when she wasn't looking.

Colton went swimming at ten o'clock that night, while Celeste stretched out on a lawn chair under the stars. The pool was partly surrounded by a huge, fake rocky ridge with caves in it. A mechanical bear and mountain lion took turns emerging from the caves and growling or screaming at intervals.

Back in the room, they watched TV a little. Colton and Celeste got to missing Smoke and worrying about him. Celeste emptied her duffel, went out to the truck, zipped Smoke up in it, and boldly rode the golden elevator up to the tenth floor. He didn't mind—the big lug. They turned out the lights, and Celeste said, "One-eyed jack. Jack of diamonds. Jack of hearts. Jack of clubs. Jack of spades."

Colton said, "Jack Daniel's, it's a kind of whiskey."

"Mmmm-hmmm."

"It helps Grandpa's hip."

"Yeah, right."

"Night, Mom."

"Night."

The next morning they snuck Smoke down to the truck early, checked out, got gas at Costco, and rumbled on over the pass, crossing the Sierra Nevada and dropping into the foothills on the west side of the range.

"What's this?" Celeste asked when she searched the bottom of her purse for her cell phone.

"Give it to Smoke," Colton told her.

"Who puts fried fish in somebody's purse?"

"It was in a napkin. It fell out."

Celeste called Frank when they got to Auburn; that was

the plan: Frank would meet them at the ranch—with Angelo LaRocca, the neighbor Frank said would help them. And they'd all unload the truck.

The sun was high, the sky was clear and blue when Colton and Celeste pulled the truck into the driveway and drove up to the house.

Frank was there, looking fit in jeans, brown leather jacket, and starched shirt, a bandanna tied around his neck. His blue eyes twinkled; his smile was bright. Frank still had an attitude about him, just what you might expect from a former fighter pilot. Celeste had told Colton that Frank was a war hero, that his plane had been shot down over the Pacific. But she hadn't heard it from him, that was for sure. Frank never talked about the war.

Colton felt guilty about being mad at Frank. He couldn't really blame him for trying to help his mom have a happier life. He just wished Frank had a farmhouse up for grabs someplace closer to Idaho Falls.

Angelo was cutting up a eucalyptus tree that had fallen between the two properties. It had squashed down the fence wire and broken a couple of posts. They all walked over to inspect the scene. Angelo lifted the face shield of his orange helmet and shook Colton's hand and Celeste's. Colton couldn't help but notice how long their eyes lingered, how long that handshake took.

But he knew his mom wasn't stupid enough to do that again.

At least he hoped not!

He checked out Angelo's chain saw: Stihl MS 280, with a twenty-inch bar.

"Gets the job done," Angelo told him. "Not too heavy, considering." He handed it to Colton. Colton tested the weight and handed it back.

He walked over and checked out the loaner pickup: black with tan leather interior, chrome wheels, and a black rack. Sweet. He had to admit, Frank had good taste when it came to trucks—and cars. Too bad he didn't want to throw his silver Jaguar in on the deal; it was parked in the driveway with the top down.

The farmhouse was freshly painted, all creamy white. Huge white calla lilies were blooming around the steps. A plum tree with purple leaves was in the yard. On the deck was a set of wicker furniture with new flowered cushions, and along the rail were colorful, empty Mexican flowerpots. "I got these for you to fill, Celeste!" Frank told her.

Then he turned to Colton. "This lady could make a rock bloom," he said.

As if Colton didn't already know that. Their house back in Idaho had looked like a jungle. And he hoped his mom would honor Colton's No-Hanging-Houseplants Rule when it came to his bedroom.

Inside, the place looked great—modern, despite the fact that the house was more than a hundred years old. There were hardwood floors with colorful, handwoven carpets in the living room, dining room, and both bedrooms.

Frank had left a few simple antique pieces of furniture: a bed and dresser in each bedroom; in the kitchen, a pine hutch and also a drop-leaf pine table and chairs. He had bought a new easy chair, ottoman, and sleeper sofa for the living room.

Frank pointed out a series of old photos on the wall by the stairway in gold, oval frames. The first was of a tall man wearing a cowboy hat, work shirt, jeans, suspenders, and boots and holding a shotgun. A woman in a long dress and apron stood beside him, frowning under her bonnet.

"They're the Parkers," said Frank. "Taylor and I found them in a box up in the rafters in the attic right after we bought the place. He framed them for me for my birthday one year."

"How nice!" said Celeste.

"Well, I asked him to," said Frank. "And he did—reluctantly. He said they gave him the willies."

Colton had to agree; the Parkers' eyes seemed to be boring straight into him. They were so intense, it looked like they could blink.

"A little ranch history lesson: Those two were the original homesteaders: Jackson and Tanya. Jackson, the poor gentleman, died in a hunting accident around the turn of the century. Late in October. Tanya dug his grave herself—up on the hill. Poor thing. On Halloween night."

Celeste said, "She did not."

"Yes, she did. Under the light of the moon. With owls hooting in the trees. And rain lightly falling."

"You are such a liar, Frank. Colton? Don't believe him. This is not history; this is fiction."

"The next one, Colton, is the original house, up by Jackson's grave."

Colton looked at the photo of the small wooden shack and the corral nearby.

"They say around Halloween the owls wake Jackson up. He rises out of his grave, walks around in the hills, drenched by the rain, calling for his wife. Taylor and I heard him one year."

"You did not," said Celeste.

"Yes we did, too."

Colton liked how Frank teased his mom. He decided to egg him on: "What did you and Taylor hear?"

"Well, since you asked I'll tell you. We were up at the spring late one night—in October. The moon was full, the owls were hooting back and forth."

"Oh, brother," mumbled Celeste. "Here we go."

"We had a fire going in an old barrel up there . . . And we saw the flames flare up, suddenly, as though wind was blowing at the base of the fire. And we heard a low, gravelly whisper—and the fire went dead out.

"First we thought we were hearing things, just scaring ourselves, and each other. But then we heard it, distinctly—whispering, like this: 'I'm c-o-l-d, Tanya,'" Frank whispered. "'So c-o-o-o-o-o-o-ld! Where a-a-a-a-re y-o-o-o-o-o-u?'"

"Gee whiz, you're so full of it," Celeste told Frank.

"So we ran into the old hunting cabin that's up there. The window was boarded up from the outside. We heard someone walking around it, rustling the leaves. And Taylor looked through the crack in the boards and saw a shadowy figure outside, arms sticking out in front of him. When Taylor looked through the crack again, there was one eyeball looking straight back at him."

Celeste put her fingers in her ears and yelled "La la la la! I'm not listening!" until Frank shut up about the ghost and went to get his trekking stick out of the Jaguar.

They toured the ranch: hay barn with a tackroom, long redwood chicken barn with a sagging roof, little old windmill slowly turning beside it, brush pile in a soggy pasture, corrugated steel outbuilding filled with rusty farm equipment, rocky hillside. And beyond it, Kingston Mountain, with grass growing on it like yellow light.

"Shall we see if we can scare up Jackson?"

"Sure," Colton said.

Frank led the way up to the old cabin. It was a long climb, and Frank steadied himself with his stick as they made their way up the hill through the trees. They stopped often to rest.

Colton could hear Angelo's chain saw buzzing below.

Finally Colton saw the boarded-up cabin with its small, rickety porch and metal roof barely visible through a stand of eucalyptus trees. In front, a few old apple trees, with lichen on the bark, grew in rows. Some were dead.

Frank unlocked the door with a skeleton key that was hidden above the door on a nail. He turned the light switch on and off a few times. "Electricity's been shut off for years," he said.

Colton looked in at the iron bed, a little old metal stool with horseshoe legs, a painted table, and two spindly, wooden chairs. A cast-iron woodstove sat in the corner, close to the wall. From between the boards on the window to the west, a shaft of light hit the floor. Dust swirled and sparkled in it.

"The folks I bought the place from swore they saw Jackson's ghost stumbling around in here, like this . . ." Frank squinted his eyes, lifted his arms straight out in front of him. "Face swollen. Eyes half shut. And his clothes all wet, shredded, hanging off him. Hat pulled down. Mouth like a big hole." He opened his mouth at Colton's mom.

She crossed her arms on her chest and looked at him.

Frank cupped his hand behind his ear. "Shhhh! Listen!"

The wind lifted the eucalyptus branches, and they sighed and creaked. A long, papery piece of eucalyptus bark fell onto the roof, and some eucalyptus seed pods rattled down onto the ground.

Frank led them around the back of the cabin. "Here's the old hand-dug well. Just an inch or two of water at the bottom, if that. It's a long way down," he said, tapping the cement lid. "And a miserable, dark, dank, lousy hole. Unless you're a cricket. You down there, Jackson?" Frank yelled. "Come on up here and meet Celeste!"

A large chink was broken out of the cement in one corner. "Should fix this. I hope no snakes slid in. Remind me to tell Angelo."

"So what was Jackson hunting?" Colton asked.

"Here we go again," mumbled Celeste.

"Bear. A bear got him before he got it."

A rock pump house with a bent metal roof stood nearby. Frank pushed open the squeaky door, and Colton peered in. Colton loved old, greasy engines; he loved the smell of motor oil in the dirt. "It's a donkey engine," Frank told him. "Just one cylinder. It doesn't run anymore."

Colton bet his dad and grandpa could get it going.

They went on to the spring. There was a shot-up, rusty fifty-gallon drum and a broken-down corral nearby, and beyond it, tall, dark, mysterious cypress trees. "The original cabin was here; you can still see part of the rock foundation. And that circle of stones, that's Jackson's final resting place."

"Oh, it is not, it's an old fire ring," Celeste told him.

The grass felt springy under Colton's feet. Water spilled out of a pool and ran between brilliant green, mossy rocks.

"Deer and raccoon," Frank said, identifying the footprints in the mud with the tip of his trekking stick. "Taylor and I saw an eagle on the ground here once. With a jackrabbit. And once we caught a glimpse of a bobcat disappearing into the trees. We've heard owls hoot, coyotes sing. It's like a Disney movie up here."

Colton listened to the water trickle and the wind lift the

branches of the eucalyptus trees, moving through the leaves like a whisper.

"After the first rains, as soon as we don't need to worry about sparks, maybe we'll all come up here and build a fire in that barrel and sit around and watch the light dance inside."

"And tell ghost stories," Colton added.

Frank looked at him. "Exactly."

Three

It took a while to unpack and settle in.

Colton and Celeste kept Smoke inside the house until his meowing became unbearable and they had to let him out. No problem; the house was set way back from the road.

Smoke had no interest in the road—just his perch on the rocky hillside, fields full of butterflies, and moths that fluttered around the porch light. Nights he slept at the end of Colton's bed, hogging it as always. Just before dawn, Smoke would wake up and want to go outside, which gave Colton a chance to straighten the covers and stretch his legs.

Then Smoke would meow at the door and Colton would let him back in.

Angelo was helpful. And handsome, Celeste had noted,

with his wide shoulders, strong arms, thick, black hair, and dark eyes. He was also knowledgeable about what to plant, and where—and when. He had an olive grove, made his own olive oil and sausages. He raised Appaloosas and blue heeler dogs. One, Lily, was pregnant, and she was missing her tail. She looked like an eggplant.

How many more heelers did Angelo need? He had four, and they moved through the grass like spirits, silently patrolling the livestock, bellies close to the ground. The only sane dog Angelo owned was Elmo, a massive Newfoundland crossed with a Saint Bernard who sat around and drooled. Big, fat head, big, wide paws. Long, slow-wagging tail. Just a great big, happy mutt: Colton's favorite kind of dog.

Angelo, Colton, and Celeste built a deer fence to protect her garden area. It was hard work, but Colton liked to work hard, and the posthole digger was fun.

Suddenly, his mom had an interest in horses. Angelo was teaching her to how to saddle up and ride. On Saturday afternoons, Celeste and Angelo sometimes went riding on the mountain and invited Colton, but Colton didn't go.

It was okay for him to ride the Appaloosas with her and Angelo but not the ponies with his dad and grandpa? What kind of sense did that make?

In any event, Colton didn't want to ride the Appaloosas with Angelo and Celeste up into the canyon to the upper lake.

School started.

It went okay.

Good, in fact.

His teacher, Mr. Viramontes, was a great guy. Colton liked his class, although one of the kids, Jared, was a pain.

Mr. Viramontes had a bonus system, so sometimes the class earned Freedom Day: games, movie, popcorn. Everyone had their own journal to write in, with lined pages and a stretchy elastic that wound around it: presents from Mr. Viramontes. And every day Colton wrote in his journal, but he didn't write much.

There wasn't much he wanted to tell. He missed sagebrush and big sky. He missed Will, Grady, their parents, his neighbors, his coach, his grandpa, Sugar, his dad—although that wasn't new. He wished his dad would call him more. That cell phone of his couldn't always be out of range! He hoped his dad would remember his birthday next May, like he didn't last year.

But he wouldn't have written any of that down. Instead, he wrote about Smoke, how he ran through the grass like a dolphin and trotted beside him like a hairy wolf.

Within a couple of weeks, Colton had made some new friends. He sat next to a girl named Monique, who was bossy, smart, loud, and nice. She had sparkly brown eyes and a whole lot of rows of pretty braids, with beads woven in.

Manuel was his best friend; he was also new to the school, from San Diego, and originally from Mexico.

Colton rode into school with a handful of other kids who lived out in the sticks, including a few from the junior high.

They shared a small van that was trying to look like a school bus: with red lights and "Arroyo District" printed on the side. An especially interesting new friend named Madison took the bus with Colton and got off at El Camino Junior High. Madison was in the seventh grade. She lived up the road from Colton. They were the first ones on and the last ones off, so they had time to get to know each other.

One warm and windy late October afternoon, Colton said goodbye to Madison and stepped off the bus.

"Monterey Jack!" shouted his mom.

Colton said nothing. He wished his mother would run out of jacks—at least when Madison could hear them.

"It's a California cheese!"

"I know, Mom."

"There's a fire in the backcountry. At first, it was coming our way, straight up the back of the mountain. But the wind shifted. Angelo says they've got it contained. So no worries at this point."

The air smelled sweet and smoky. Colton looked to the east, where a thick cloud of pale yellow smoke hung in the sky high above Madison's house. He could see the red lights of the bus flashing as it stopped in the mouth of her driveway, where a big truck was parked. "What makes him so sure?"

"Been listening to his radio. He's a volunteer firefighter, you realize."

Angelo this, Angelo that.

"Mom?" Colton said, as they headed to the house. "I really

am good to get off the bus at the end of my driveway and walk five hundred feet home in broad daylight."

"I know, sweetie. But I look forward to meeting you," she said. "Okay?"

"Sure."

One of Angelo's peacocks had hopped the fence and come visiting; he fanned his tail and strutted around at the end of the driveway. He shook his feathers, then belted out his characteristic loud, harsh scream.

Colton wished he'd take his feathery rear back to where he belonged.

"So how was your day?" Celeste asked.

"Good. We're doing wildlife reports, and everybody gets to pick an animal."

"Well, that's right up your alley!"

"I know! And our class had so many bonus points we got to watch an old movie. *Ghostbusters*."

"I remember that one. Scary!"

"Oh, Mom." Colton gave her a look. "Anyway, Mr. Viramontes picked Manuel and me for Students of the Month."

"Congratulations!"

Colton watch Smoke approaching. "Well, I don't think it's because we're the best students. I think it's because we're the newest ones."

"How new is Manuel?"

"As new as me."

"Catch."

Celeste reached into her pocket and tossed him an apple.

Colton took a bite. "I'm supposed to bring in pictures and stuff."

"Well, I put everything to do with photos in the hutch. Why don't you start there? The album's in the drawer," said Celeste. "And there's more in a basket on top."

Colton leaned down to scratch Smoke's head, and Smoke followed him inside. Colton finished the apple and made a three-pointer into the trash basket on the other side of the kitchen.

Then he snuck a piece of turkey out of a package in the fridge and gave it to Smoke.

Colton stopped to check out the L.L.Bean catalog that had come in the mail for Frank. He liked that one; he'd read it later.

Colton pulled open the heavy wooden drawer of the hutch. He took out the familiar flat photo album and put it on the kitchen table. There were lots of empty spaces in the first few pages. Colton wished his mom hadn't gone through and taken out all the pictures of his dad and her, back in the day. The pretty casino girl and her handsome cowboy, leaning against a fence rail—that one was gone. And the picture from the wedding chapel was also gone.

Colton flipped to the hospital photo: Celeste in the bed with her bangs stuck to her face, smiling; his dad in a green gown beside her, holding Colton just moments after he was born. Should he bring it? No. His face looked like a pancake with two blueberries stuck in it.

Colton looked at pictures taken at JCPenneys when

he was a baby, some from the Little Red Schoolhouse Preschool, and then, in order, the school pictures, kindergarten through fifth grade. Two for the third grade, since he'd done that grade twice. In last year's class picture—from Mrs. Barron's class—Colton was standing between Will and Grady, the Trouble Trio, Mrs. Barron called them. She didn't mean it, though.

Colton turned the page. Oh, boy. There it was: the classic that his grandpa took with a Polaroid. His dad and him on Sugar. They were wearing twin shirts, with white pearl snaps and arrows on the pockets. Both of them were grinning. Colton was missing his two front teeth.

If his dad hadn't also been missing his front teeth in the picture, he'd have brought that one in for the display. But when his mom volunteered at school, she sometimes stopped by his classroom. That was just about the last picture she'd want to see pinned up on the wall.

Next?

Yup. There they were: mom, dad, and kid, taken with a timer at Old Faithful in Yellowstone National Park. Colton's dad stood tall in his white straw hat and cowboy boots, wearing Wranglers and a rodeo belt buckle as big as a plate. You couldn't read what it said, but Colton knew it by heart: PROFESSIONAL RODEO COWBOYS ASSOCIATION, JESSE HUDSON, NATIONAL CHAMPION BULL RIDER. His dad had two of those.

His arm was slung around Celeste. She was holding Colton. The geyser was erupting behind them.

Old Faithful?

Colton looked at his dad.

Maybe not.

He wished he could remember the day that picture was taken. He wished he could remember when they were a family of three.

The screen door opened, and Colton's mom walked in. She took off her red rubber gardening clogs. "Finding everything okay?"

"Yup."

Colton flipped the page. He found a picture of Smoke, the big oaf, stretched on a black ottoman. Black against black: all you could see were his eyes. And Colton decided on a snapshot of Frank when he was a fighter pilot, with his hand resting on the propeller of a Grumman Hellcat. Yeah, he was mad at Frank for instigating the move out to California, but he still looked up to him, respected him. Frank was a World War II veteran. Sure he was proud of Frank.

"Please make sure you put the pictures back in the right places after the Student of the Month display comes down," Celeste told him.

"I know, Mom," said Colton.

He looked up at her. You should talk, he thought. He wondered where Celeste had put the pictures of her and his dad together—or had she just thrown them out?

"What?" she asked him.

"Nothing."

Colton looked through the "Vacation" envelope in the

basket and chose one: mom and kid standing on a lookout on the rim of the Grand Canyon. The Grand Canyon at dusk. Colton had never seen anything so empty in his life. But he supposed it would do.

Last photo: his uncle Chad in his Air Force uniform standing between his grandpa and his dad. Colton hadn't spent much time with his uncle Chad, but he liked what he knew of him. Three peas in a pod: tall, wide shoulders, big grins. Grandpa had shrunk an inch or two over the years and lost some weight, but all three in the picture stood over six feet tall.

But there were four Hudson boys. And Colton planned to surpass them. Just give him a few years.

He had two pairs of too-short Wrangler jeans in his drawer that had fit him fine before they came out to California. His mom had to get him some bigger ones, longer ones—much longer.

Colton put away the basket and the album, picked up the catalog, photos, and his pack, and headed upstairs. His bedroom was still so fresh and neat. It hadn't really become his yet. He looked on the dresser. What else could he choose for the display?

Little old pink piggy?

No way.

Baseball trophy?

No. Don't show off.

Pictionary game?

No. But he was good at that, if he did say so himself.

He opened his closet door. Now there was a mess! He stared down at his cowboy boots. It had been a while since he'd worn them; he wondered if they still fit. He picked up one and looked at it, at the sole with holes and the worn undershot heel. A lot of good rides on Sugar in those.

On the shelf above was his white straw hat. He hadn't worn that lately, either.

Colton still hadn't figured out the California style—if there was one. T-shirts and jeans worked. He wasn't sure how many of the other boys bought their jeans at the hardware store.

He picked up the shot-up license plate. It had the silhouette of a cowboy riding a bucking bronco, with his arm in the air, holding up a hat.

Perfect.

Later on, he snuck back downstairs and took the Polaroid of him and his dad on Sugar for safekeeping. He took the Old Faithful picture, too. He stuck them between the pages of his math book with the other photos, in case he changed his mind.

Four

Madison patted the empty seat beside her, and Colton sat down: two in one seat, with the whole rest of the bus empty, but oh well. It was fine with Colton, as long as his mom didn't see.

Madison helped herself to the license plate sticking out of Colton's pack. "What's this?"

"It's for Student of the Month," Colton told her.

"Who shot it all up?"

"I don't know."

"What else have you got?"

Colton pulled out his math book and showed Madison the photos. Not all of them.

"That's a cat?"

"Yup. Smoke."

"Whoa. It's huge!"

"I know."

"What does it eat?"

"Kitty Kibbles and bugs."

"I have a goldfish who got fat like that, eating bugs."

"Smoke is all muscle," said Colton. "He works out chasing butterflies."

"What a hunk . . . I just love cats," said Madison with a sigh. "And I really really want a kitten. Of course I can't have one, though, because my big brother Gavin's allergic. So I had to settle for a goldfish: the Stinkman." She brightened. "But we're getting rid of him soon."

"The Stinkman?"

"No, Gavin. My dad rented a truck, and he's moving Gavin and all his stuff to Boston. They're taking their time getting there. Sightseeing. Going through the parks."

I hope they get a truck with bucket seats, Colton thought to himself.

"Gavin's going to work at my uncle's camera store. And he and my cousins are starting a band. He plays drums. And keyboard. You should see all the stuff they have to pack up. Cool plane," Madison said. "Who's he?"

"My mom's great-uncle. He's eighty something, and he drives a Jaguar."

"He does?"

Colton watched as Madison dug in her pack and took out a bar of soap. "I'm working on this in my art class! It looks like a van, but it is soon to be a classic Porsche."

Colton nodded his approval. He liked it that Madison carved race cars out of soap. And named a fish the Stinkman. In fact, Colton liked everything about Madison: her fast smile, that she was tall, funny, strong. That she laughed with her eyes.

The bus driver stopped at the railroad tracks, opened the door, and listened. A huge black bull was standing behind the fence, eating a broken pumpkin.

"What are you going to be for Halloween?" Madison asked.

"Nothing. What about you?"

"I don't know yet. Gavin thinks I should be a chewed-up piece of bubble gum. Or a boxer with a bloody nose. But I better hurry up and decide. My school's having a Halloween dance. With a DJ. I'm on the decorating committee. Guess what I'm in charge of."

"What?"

"A six-foot-tall black papier-mâché cat with light-up yellow eyes. My mom and dad are making it. Actually, Mom's making the whole thing. She's so stressed out, with Dad leaving. And Gavin moving out. And she also has to bake six dozen sugar cookies shaped like ghosts."

"What's a ghost cookie shaped like?"

"A sheet with air in it, I guess."

Madison asked Colton, "Do you believe in ghosts?"

He answered, "Do you?"

"Well, sort of."

Colton smiled a little to himself. "There's a ghost that

haunts the cabin above where we live, up on the hill. With a big ol' cowboy hat and boots, and a hole for a mouth. And his jacket all torn to shreds."

"Yeah. I've heard about him. Everybody on Kingston Mountain has. Gavin says he saw him. Said he saw him walking around in the shadows, under the trees, whispering to himself. Gavin's such a liar. I'm glad he's going to Boston."

"Was the ghost whispering 'I'm co-o-o-old'?" whispered Colton.

Madison looked sideways at Colton. "Why do you ask?"

"Because my mom's great-uncle saw him up there, too. He did."

"Not," said Madison.

"Was he wearing a shredded-up jacket with a bent-up hat brim when your brother saw him?"

As the bus stopped at the junior high, Madison found a small dead beetle on the rim of the window. "Here, Colt," she said. "Give it to Smoke, from me."

He loved it that Madison called him Colt. He also liked it that she wasn't afraid of bugs. He was glad he lived far away from school so he could ride with Madison. He liked that she sort of believed in ghosts, because maybe he could scare her sometime.

Colton watched as Madison disappeared into a crowd of kids. If he hadn't done third grade twice, he'd have gotten off the bus back there with Madison. He'd be in the junior high with her. That would have been good.

But if he hadn't done third grade twice, he wouldn't be caught up on reading. Sort of. He still needed extra help, and he was good with that. He knew how fast you read wasn't a measure of intelligence. He liked to read, he just read slowly. He liked the catalogs that piled up at the ranch for Frank. He liked car magazines. And he liked books, too—especially books with lots of pictures. He liked atlases, maps. He was getting help in reading from Ms. Jensen, who also worked part-time in the library. He liked Ms. Jensen; she was originally from Montana. Lately, she'd been telling Colton about ranching college, which interested him.

When he wasn't in school, Colton called Ms. Jensen by her first name, Louise. That was because Louise and his mom had become friends. The friendship had started when his mom volunteered to reshelve books once a week in the library. Louise lived just a few miles from Colton and Celeste. They also discovered that they both had a passion for gardening. Sometimes Louise stopped by for tea. She called it a Gardening Gabfest. She usually brought along homemade cookies or muffins. All healthy ingredients—but not too bad, considering.

Louise had been out sick for a few days, and Colton missed her. He liked reading with her. When she came back, he'd talk her into helping him with his wildlife report.

The bus pulled up along the curb behind the bigger buses that brought the kids who lived in town. Colton got out. He watched Manuel boot his soccer ball around; the bell rang. Everybody went inside.

He and Manuel gave Mr. Viramontes their Student of the Month stuff and sat down. After attendance and announcements, the kids in the class began searching through a pile of books and magazines for topics for their wildlife reports. There were three computers with Internet access in the classroom; Daniela, Liliana, and Monique were using them. Hogging them, actually—as usual.

Colton pored over the wildlife pictures in a brand-new book—*California Wildlife: Then and Now*—while Mr. Viramontes arranged the Student of the Month display.

Colton didn't care about the girls hogging the computers because he preferred looking at the photos and drawings in *California Wildlife: Then and Now*. He wasn't sure what his report should be about. He needed something in the "now" category. But he checked out the "thens" anyway: No more grizzlies left in California—sad, but maybe not a completely bad thing. He stopped at a drawing of a snarling wolverine: another noble animal gone from California that Colton thought was awesome yet wouldn't have wanted slinking into his camp.

Next page: Nows. Mountain lions, a.k.a. cougars—still alive and well in the backcountry in various places throughout the state of California. And lately they'd been making a comeback. Colton stared at the photo. The cat stared back, with yellow eyes—like Smoke's. The caption read: "Mountain lions are quiet, solitary, and evasive. They typically avoid people. Mountain lion attacks are extremely rare.

However, conflicts are increasing as California's human population expands into mountain lion habitats."

Manuel was also looking at books about mountain lions. He showed Colton a book written in Spanish: *Pumas*. They leafed through the pictures together, stopping at a close-up of an awesome puma drinking from a spring in moonlight —with water drizzling out of its mouth. Colton noted its fangs and the thick black line around its lips.

"Let's draw," suggested Manuel.

They each worked on a pencil drawing from the photo of the big cat drinking from the spring. Manuel showed Colton how to leave a small patch of white in each eyeball, to make it look like light in the lens.

Jared watched over Manuel's shoulder. "That's copying," he accused.

Colton and Manuel said nothing. Jared had skipped a grade, which may have been a mistake. He was too young for the grade he was supposed to be in to begin with. He had a big mouth for such a little guy. Colton didn't know what made Jared act like Jared, but he figured he'd grow out of it, sooner or later. He hoped so, anyway.

Mr. Viramontes strolled over. "Both doing pumas? Great! Do you want to partner up for this project?"

"They're copying," said Jared.

"How else can you draw a puma?" said Mr. Viramontes.

The boys kept working until Mr. Viramontes announced that it was time to put the reference materials away.

"But I didn't get my turn on the computer!" said Jared. "I need an image of a wild boar."

"There are plenty of images of boars in the books in the classroom. Refer to those and draw one," Mr. Viramontes told him.

"I don't want to draw one! I want to print one out!" Jared protested.

"Jared? The computer lab is open during lunch recess," Mr. Viramontes said. "As you well know. Ask Ms. Jensen about wild boars."

Good, thought Colton. She was back!

"Okay then," said Mr. Viramontes. "Students of the Month! Who wants to go first?"

Manuel pointed to Colton.

"Talk to us, Colton. Tell us about the photos. Come on up here."

Colton went to the display. "That's my dad, Grandpa, and Dad's brother—my uncle Chad. He's a fighter pilot. And there's Mom's great-uncle and the plane he used to fly." He could have said Frank could take it off from an aircraft carrier and land it—at night.

"Then, there's me and my mom at the Grand Canyon. And my cat, Smoke."

"Big guy!" said Mr. Viramontes.

"Twenty pounds."

Mr. Viramontes whistled.

"Me and my grandpa found that Wyoming license plate near his ranch in Idaho."

Colton could have said, "And the bronc rider on the plate reminds me of my dad, who's a rodeo cowboy—a champion bull rider."

"Anything else you want to share?"

Colton wasn't much of a talker. "Not really."

"Well, thank you, Colton."

The kids clapped.

"Manuel? You're up. Who's this?"

On Manuel's side of the bulletin board, there was a photo and a cap. The photo was of a middle-aged couple smiling under a sign that said "Mi Pueblo." "That's my dad's uncle Alberto and his aunt Cleo, in front of their restaurant downtown. And that's my dad's Pumas hat. Our favorite team. From Mexico."

Manuel paused.

"Anything else?"

"Not really."

Mr. Viramontes picked up a black-and-white soccer ball from the ball bin. It had "Manuel" written on it in felt-tip marker. "What about this?"

"On weekends I play soccer at el Parque de los Patos."

"Spring Lake Park is also known as Parque de los Patos," Mr. Viramontes told the class. "Duck Park. Who plays?"

"My family."

"Anything else you want to share?"

"My dad played semipro in Mexico. His uncle Alberto did, too. When he was young."

Manuel looked at Colton. "But they're also cowboys. My grandpa has a ranch in Mexico."

Mr. Viramontes asked, "Whereabouts?"

"Near San Felipe."

"Ah. Pretty place. I've been there."

Manuel headed back to his desk. The class clapped, and Manuel sat down.

"Just so you know," said Mr. Viramontes, "I can relate to Manuel's attachment to his soccer ball. Back when I was playing soccer, I took my soccer ball everywhere with me. I even slept with it."

"*That*," said Jared, "is ridiculous."

"Think so? Do you sleep with a stuffed animal?"

"No. I sleep with my dog Shorty."

"What kind of dog?"

"Jack Russell terrier."

Colton would have to remember that jack. That was a good one.

Mr. Viramontes looked around the room. "How many others here sleep with a pet?"

A few students raised their hands.

"How many get woken up all night long, with the pet sprawled in the middle of the bed?" He paused. "How many wake up hugging the edge of the mattress? And freezing? Pull on the covers, can't get them up around you—because the blankets are pinned under the animal?"

Colton could have raised his hand on any one of those.

"Well, my friends, some people would think *that* is ridiculous. Sleeping with a soccer ball is much more comfortable. A soccer ball sits quietly all night long on a pillow."

Jared challenged Mr. Viramontes. "Do you sleep with a pet?"

"My dog Luke used to sleep at the foot of my bed and snore, yes. But I have something else I'd like to share at the moment, something more about soccer.

"When I was in the fifth grade, my family moved to a new town. In the beginning, I didn't have many friends. My parents both worked and were busy and tired at the end of the day. So I was lonely a lot of the time. My teacher suggested that I go to the soccer practices after school. I hadn't played much, but it didn't take me long to develop some skills. Then, soccer became my life. It helped me develop confidence. I learned that hard work pays off. Best of all, I made lifelong friends. I would recommend the game to anyone."

"So," said Jared, "why don't you coach? You got so much from the game; now it's time to give back. My dad told me the soccer league gets filled up because there aren't enough coaches."

"Would he consider coaching? I can put him in touch with a friend of mine who—"

"No, he doesn't play team sports. He likes to hike. And do yoga."

"That works."

"But you do! Maybe Manuel wants to be on a team. Colton's new, like you were. Maybe he wants to be on a soccer team. Ever think of that?"

"Jared? You're full of advice this morning. You should put up a sign: advice, ten cents. However, I've got quite a bit on my plate. Do you know I just signed up to help make two hundred tamales for the Día de los Muertos parade?"

"Can you make two hundred and twenty and bring us some?"

"We'll see."

Manuel turned to Colton and quietly told him, "We are cowboys in my family."

Colton took out his math book and flipped through the pages. "This is me and my dad."

Manuel looked at the picture. "Nice horse."

"Her name is Sugar."

Colton closed the photo back up in the book.

"Do you and your dad want to play soccer on Saturday?" Manuel asked.

"My dad doesn't live around here. I didn't play that much soccer in Idaho." Colton could have said that baseball was his game, that he was on All Stars for the past two years, had pitched a no-hitter, and was voted Player of the Year back in Idaho Falls.

"That's okay, man," said Manuel. "Come to el Parque de los Patos at two o'clock."

Five

Smoke lay on the couch beside Colton, with his eyes halfway closed and one front leg slung over the cushion. Talk about a couch hog. Colton was squeezed up against the arm. He scratched behind Smoke's ears while Celeste cooked pasta. There was a big wad of fur with a burr stuck in it. He'd have to cut it out somehow, if Smoke would let him, which wasn't likely.

The pasta smelled good: fettuccine Alfredo. But Colton wondered: What ever happened to mac and cheese?

Lately, ever since Angelo came onto the scene, Celeste was remembering everything she forgot from culinary school. Colton even heard her talk about opening a restaurant in town.

California cuisine: pasta this and pasta that. Some of it was green!

Colton would also have been happy with some spaghetti and meatballs from the Wagon Wheel, with garlic bread. And Parmesan in the shiny green can, not fresh grated anything.

"You didn't tell me," Celeste called from the kitchen, "how did the Student of the Month thing go for you and Manuel?"

"Good. Manuel and I are also doing our wildlife report together—on pumas. Or cougars, whatever. Mountain lions. Anyway, don't forget, we're playing soccer on Saturday at the park."

"I won't. And I'd like to meet his family."

"Mom? It's a soccer game."

"Right. But I'm not going to drop you off at a public park without even knowing who's supervising. And, Colton? I wish just once on a weekend you'd ride with Angelo and me."

Colton said nothing.

"What else is going on in the classroom these days?"

"Monique is planning our Halloween party. She put me on the committee."

"See? I told you. You'll make lots of new friends here. What's your committee in charge of?"

"Cleanup."

"Ah."

"What are you going to be for Halloween?"

"I'm twelve, Mom."

"I would have enjoyed making a costume for you. Remember when you were Batman?"

"Yup."

"Did you like that costume?"

"Yup."

"Your classmate Jared helped me reshelve books the other day. He's going to be a Maytag repairman for Halloween."

Colton was quiet.

Then he said: "Jackass, Mom."

And she said: "Jack-o'-lantern."

And he said: "Jumping jack."

"Jack Russell terrier—it's a dog."

"Dang! I know that, Mom. Jackson Parker—it's a ghost."

"Set the table."

After supper, Colton helped clean up and they sat in the living room and watched a program on PBS about black bears. Smoke watched, too, growling occasionally.

"That's what Jackson was hunting when he died," Colton told Celeste. "A big ol' bear.

"I'm c-o-o-o-old!" he whispered under his breath. "Halloween's coming right on up, Mom! Time for Jackson's ghost to make an appearance. But don't worry, I got your back."

"Yeah, I know."

They watched a bear rummaging through the back of an

SUV while the owner stood helplessly at a distance. The back door to the SUV had been pulled off the hinges and was lying on the ground.

"Once, right after your father and I got married, he took me camping in a campground not far from Reno called French Camp. There was a sign to watch out for bears. We built a big fire and sat around it. A fire will keep any wild animal away.

"Course your father told bear stories. When we went to bed, we put the fire out with a big bucket of water. I suggested filling the bucket with utensils and bringing it into our tent to shake in case any wild animals came around."

Colton yawned.

"But no, no. Your father said that wasn't necessary. It wasn't grizzly territory, and he said he couldn't care less about black bears.

"Of course, once we were in the tent, he made growling and scratching sounds. He's worse than Frank, in his own way.

"But in the middle of the night he got a surprise: a bear really did come around. It tore the door off the camper top and crawled in, and ate a case of Top Ramen and washed it down with eighteen cans of beer. While your father stood outside the tent hollering—in his shorts."

Colton wished Celeste wouldn't call his dad "your father." His name was Dad. Or Jesse. And she knew it.

He got up and went into the bathroom to wash his face and brush his teeth.

What?

In the sink, there was an assortment of dead beetles, flies, ants—and a huge dead mosquito hawk lying on its back with its legs folded up. Smoke was sitting on the edge of the sink. A moth wing was dangling from his one white whisker. "What happened here?" Colton called.

His mother appeared in the doorway. "Oh. I changed the lightbulb and those fell out of the fixture. I forgot to clean them up."

Colton took Smoke out onto the porch. They plopped into a wicker chair.

The same round moon was up above his grandpa's ranch in Idaho, and Colton wouldn't be surprised if he was looking at it—like he said.

He wondered if his dad saw it, too—wherever he was tonight.

He heard the screen door squeak open and bang shut. His mom came out. "Everything going okay, Colton?"

"Yup. Why?"

"Just making sure."

And everything was okay—good, in fact.

And just about to get better.

At school the next morning, Mr. Viramontes called Colton and Manuel up to his desk. "I admit it," he began. "Jared guilted me out. I e-mailed a counselor over at the junior high who's been very involved with the soccer league, and Jared is correct."

Again? Colton thought.

"The teams are full. But," continued Mr. Viramontes, "he said if any openings came up, he'd let us know."

"Okay, good," said Manuel.

"The plot thickens. This morning I opened my e-mail, and lookee here."

Colton looked at the screen.

From: Dino Ruffoni. To: a long list of people, including George Viramontes. Subject line: INJURIES, ETC.

Mr. Viramontes began reading out loud:

To parents, friends, and players:

We had a couple of injuries yesterday, unrelated to soccer. Max: Sprained knee—scooter mishap. Ryan: broke his wrist—skateboarding accident. We do wish these boys a speedy recovery. Under the circumstances, we need to add one player, possibly two. I'd like to do a head count as to who can make it to practice and the next game. Please let me know.

Dino Ruffoni

226 Turtle Lane

707.795.5555

Also: We have the following in the lost and found:

A sweatshirt labeled WANTED: SOMEONE TO DO MY HOMEWORK AND CHORES.

Mr. Viramontes asked Manuel: "Interested?"

"Sure."

"Can you get over to fill out the application? Ask your dad. Tell him this coach is a friend of mine and a very good guy. A champion. Played in Europe and here. Great, great coach."

"Okay."

"Does he have e-mail?"

"My uncle does."

"Dad have a cell phone?"

"Yes."

"It's Enrique, right? What's the number?"

Manuel told him.

"Colton? You in?"

Why not? thought Colton. Because you stink at soccer! he told himself.

"Yeah, sure. But I haven't played that much."

"That's okay. Got to start somewhere, right? Talk to Dino. I'll forward this e-mail to your mom," he added. "It has all the contact info."

"I can get an application for both of us," Colton told Manuel. "I'll bring yours to the park."

"There ya go!"

After dinner, Colton's mom e-mailed the coach. Then they drove into town, into a subdivision with pretty yards. Celeste parked the truck in front of 226 Turtle Lane, and they got out and knocked on the door.

Dino's wife, Teresa, answered. Celeste introduced herself

and Colton. They heard shouting coming from downstairs: "Let's go, Italy!"

Teresa said, "That's Dino. Very enthusiastic! He's been replaying the soccer highlights from the World Cup 2006 for our daughters."

They heard loud whistling and clapping.

"Dino!" she called. "They're here!"

Dino bounded up the steps. He was holding twin baby girls, one on each hip. "We've been watching the team with the best defense in the world! Right, girls?"

They stared at him.

"This is . . . Marisa. And this is . . . Angie. I'm Dino."

Colton told everybody hi.

Celeste said, "Adorable! Times two."

"Thanks. We agree."

Dino passed one of the babies to Teresa.

"So George Viramontes is your teacher. He's quite a guy. Great player, back in the day. Do you two have a few minutes?"

They all sat down.

"Did George tell you the story about how he used to sleep with his soccer ball when he was a kid?"

"Yup."

"Yeah, soccer's great, but family and friends are important, too. We always keep it in perspective. Sometimes we have a come one, come all get-together: kids, teens, adults, grandmas and grandpas. Called Soccer Time. We hang out, talk about stuff. Eat great food and play soccer. I think of it as soccer therapy.

"My other job is school counselor," he said, as an aside.

"And then we also have scrimmages where it's fine to bring along a friend or family member who likes to play.

"Actual soccer practices are more serious. The pace is fast. You work hard, improve on weak points. Practices are short: one hour. We keep it upbeat. Get in, work hard, go home—relax, recuperate, and stay strong mentally. Be fresh for the games."

"Sounds good," Colton said, then added, "I haven't played much."

"That doesn't matter. Our main goal is to teach everybody how to handle the soccer ball, play different positions. Like Reyna would say, Play first, win later."

Celeste smiled at Teresa, holding one of the babies, listening. "So beautiful!"

"Thank you."

"How old?"

"Ten months."

Dino told Colton, "Bring sweats and sweatshirts for practice. If you guys want to practice in the goal, be sure to wear long pants, sweatpants, and shin guards—because you'll be on and off the ground.

"Jerseys need numbers on both the yellow and blue. R & S Sports out on Fifth Street can put on the numbers, but we'll figure that out later. Got a soccer ball?"

"We'll get one," Celeste said.

"That's all you need for now. Welcome to the team."

Dino gave Colton two applications, two copies of "Healthy Snack Suggestions," two Soccer Facts sheets, two player questionnaires, and two soccer ball key chains.

"Let's play soccer! The beautiful game, as Pelé calls it. Right, Angie?" Angie extended one drooly hand to Celeste, and Celeste held it for a moment.

"So soft!" Celeste closed her eyes and smiled. "I'd love to have another one of these . . . or two . . ."

She would? That was news to Colton!

"Lucky you!" said Celeste.

"Yup," said Dino. "We hit the jackpot okay."

Six

After Colton and his mom got home, they sat awhile on the porch with Smoke. Elmo came over and plopped down, too. Then Lily. The other heelers were too busy patrolling to relax. Lily was slowing down. She soon fell asleep.

Sitting on the porch with the Pet Posse was getting to be a tradition.

Below, Colton could hear the faraway sound of a train whistle, the lonesomest sound in the world.

"Where does that train go?" he asked. "Is it a passenger train, or a freight? Think it goes to Idaho?"

Celeste didn't know.

Colton said good night and carried Smoke up the stairs to

his room, stopping for a moment to check out the photo of Jackson and Tanya.

Truth was, the Parkers were scary. For real. Especially Jackson. He had a crazy look about him. Tanya looked like a female version of Oscar the Grouch. Maybe it was just the photo.

Colton was glad he had Smoke to keep him company.

When he got back to Idaho, he'd tell his grandpa the Jackson Parker story. See if he could raise a few hairs on the back of his neck.

Colton was excited about soccer. He looked forward to the challenge. He liked Dino's style. Liked his attitude about sports. The way Colton saw it, Soccer Time wasn't all that different from a bunch of people getting together to barbecue and play horseshoes. Nobody thought of it as horseshoes therapy back in Idaho Falls, but this was California.

Scrimmages sounded like fun. Colton bet Manuel would bring Enrique and Uncle Alberto sometime. They'd have a few things to show the team.

Did Madison play sports?

Maybe she'd come, too. He pictured her face. Remembered their conversation. He repeated it in his mind and drifted off to sleep.

In the middle of the night, Smoke stood on the pillow close to Colton's head. He stared down at Colton and blinked. A moment later, he leaped onto the bookshelf: a puff of black smoke that took the shape of a barn owl, blacker than the sky beyond the window behind him. He meowed, a tiny meow for such a big guy. Colton knew that he wanted out, just for a while. Smoke wanted to explore the black, windy grass and empty barns. And the rocky hillside behind them.

Colton could relate to that.

He followed Smoke down the stairs and opened the door. Smoke paused on the threshold and looked out. Then he walked into the darkness.

Back upstairs, it felt good to stretch out. The bigger Colton got, the smaller that bed got, especially with Smoke sprawled in the middle of it. But for some reason Colton tossed and turned.

He got up a few hours later with an uneasy feeling. Smoke wasn't back yet.

He went downstairs and opened the door. "Smoke. Are you out there?" he whispered. But all he heard was an owl hoot. All he saw in the dim light were the huge white calla lilies blooming in the dark by the side of the porch stairs.

Colton went back up to his room. But he couldn't sleep. He turned on his light and leafed through the L.L.Bean catalog. That woke him up even more.

He got up, took the plastic stopper out of the bottom of his piggy bank, and pulled out all the money. Eighty dollars, enough for a trekking stick for his grandpa, with two different tips, and enough to cover the tax.

He tore out the order form and envelope, found a pencil, and filled it out, then put the cash in the envelope. But when he reviewed everything, he noticed it said "No cash" on the form.

Dang! Why not?

Well, he'd figure it out somehow. He tucked it all under his mattress; that was where his grandpa kept his valuables. Including his own grandpa's gold railroad watch.

As soon as it was light, Colton got dressed. He went and stood in the tall grass by the hay barn and whistled. Celeste came outside in her robe and slippers. "What's up?" she asked.

"Smoke didn't come home."

Celeste walked down the driveway, clapping her hands. "Smoke? Where are you, partner?"

Colton went into the barn. He climbed the wooden ladder to the loft. He looked around in the hay bales. Then he unlatched the big door under the peak of the roof and swung it open.

He saw nothing below but an empty field full of thistles going to seed.

Colton walked upward between the rocks and oaks on the hill behind the barn, whistling and calling Smoke's name. Maybe Smoke was up on his lookout: the tallest boulder in the field. He wasn't.

From the top, Colton could see Angelo's spotted Appaloosas grazing on the hillside. Maybe Smoke had gone to Angelo's, although Colton doubted it; Smoke didn't like those hyper heelers much. Except Lily. And he didn't mind Elmo, either. Smoke and Elmo were the same type: big guys. Low-key. Maybe they were hanging out over there together: the Pet Posse.

Celeste got dressed, and they walked over to Angelo's. She knocked on the door. "Have you seen Smoke? He didn't come back last night."

Angelo hadn't, but he said, "Come on in."

Colton looked around the room; three rifles were in a locked cabinet. On the wall was an oil painting, a landscape of a vineyard with a table in the middle, piled with food and bottles of wine.

"I need to cancel out of the ride," Colton's mom told Angelo. "And I've been wondering: Would Elmo chase Smoke away somewhere?"

"Him?" Angelo asked. Elmo was sprawled on the rug.

"Would the heelers?"

"They're working dogs, Celeste," Angelo told her. "They herd cattle; they don't chase cats. They've been around Smoke before—you and Colton know that.

"But, Celeste?" he said quietly. "Let me look along the road. I saw some headlights out there late last night, heard cars racing."

As Angelo drove up and down the road, pulling over to search in the grass alongside, Colton and his mom went home. After a while, he pulled into their driveway and parked. Colton's heart thumped as Angelo slowly got out. He leaned into the pickup bed and lifted up something heavy.

It was a flat of flowers.

"Nothing in the ditch but weeds. And McDonald's wrappers up by the overlook," he reported.

He set the flowers on the porch. "I've been meaning to bring you these," he told Celeste.

"Why, thank you, Angelo. Pretty, aren't they, Colton?"

Colton didn't want to talk about flowers. "Think Smoke could be shut in somewhere over at your place? What about the tack room?"

"I'll look. And I'll check around up by the hunting cabin," Angelo said. "And up in all those cypress branches, by the spring—in case Smoke got treed by a raccoon or something."

"You and I can talk to the neighbors," Celeste told Colton. They got into the truck and headed up the winding road. "That's nice of Angelo to be so concerned, isn't it?"

Colton didn't want to talk about how nice Angelo was. "Smoke would never go all the way up here, Mom. He always sticks around the house."

"Okay. But at least we can say hello and they can be on the lookout."

They pulled into Madison's driveway.

"I wonder who lives here," Celeste ventured.

Colton played dumb.

Nobody was home. The truck was gone. They continued up the road to the mansion on the ridgeline. "You never know about a cat," said his mother. "And I've been meaning to introduce myself to these folks regardless." They drove up a wide, white cement driveway. A couple of new cars were parked in front of the garage. They heard a low bark.

Colton and Celeste got out of the truck and rang the doorbell on the side of the house. A woman answered, holding a Chihuahua.

"Hello there," said Colton's mom. "We're your new neighbors—from way down there. We're looking for a huge Maine coon cat—black, with yellow eyes."

"One white whisker," added Colton.

"Would you like to come in?" the woman said. There were dog toys scattered everywhere. The head of a huge Great Dane filled a doggie door on the other side of the room. "That's Brutus," she said. "He can't fit." He woofed, then whined. "Go on!" she told Brutus. "Beat it!" Brutus pulled his head out. Then poked it back in again.

"Go get 'em, Cindy!" She put the Chihuahua on the linoleum. "Show him who's boss!"

The Chihuahua raced through the rubber flap into the backyard, yipping.

"Brutus just keeps growing and growing. No surprise—that's his job. A couple of days ago he cleared that six-foot redwood fence and came back all muddy. We have to call a fencer up here to figure out how to make it taller. Maybe a little lattice. Can't let a dog roam these hills, no way! Dogs get to chasing the livestock, running them ragged, and the ranchers won't tolerate that. Not that Brutus would hurt a fly, bless his pea-pickin' heart. He's a big dope is all he is.

Just a big goofball. But we were talking about cats. No. Haven't seen any cats. Who should I call if I do?"

Celeste wrote down their number.

"Welcome to the neighborhood," said the woman. "My husband, Jim, hounded me for ten years to move up here, and finally I gave in. This morning I went out to the trash can to throw out a figurine Jim broke and saw a gray fur hat at the bottom. I thought, Who would throw away a nice fur hat? Then it opened its mouth and hissed at me. It was a possum—and I tipped over the can and shooed it away. I can't believe Jim broke that figurine! Darn him anyway!"

Celeste gave her a sympathetic look.

"Men!" said the woman.

She winked at Colton. "Only kidding," she told him.

They thanked the woman and said goodbye.

"Jeeze peas," mumbled Celeste once they got back into the truck. She pulled onto the road. "What time are you supposed to meet Manuel at the park?"

"Two, but I'm not going."

"Yes you are! Manuel will worry if you don't show up. So we go and say you can't stay. And he may need those papers before Monday."

"Okay, Mom!"

"Colton Hudson? Don't raise your voice. You're not the only one worried about Smoke."

At home, Celeste called the Humane Society. She listened to the found pets hotline recording. Then she pushed a button on the phone and spoke with a volunteer. She described

Smoke and asked if they had a cat that fit his description. They didn't but took down the information and told her to keep checking the hotline and to come by on Monday to look through the found book for herself. "Well, he hasn't even been gone a day," his mother told the volunteer. "I'm sure he'll show up."

"You are?" Colton asked her when she hung up the phone.

"Well, pretty much . . ." said Celeste.

They left for the park at one-thirty. It wasn't hard to find Manuel, who was watching for them. He waved and ran over when they drove up. Colton lowered the window. "I can't stay. I need to find my cat. He took off."

"The big one? That's too bad, man," said Manuel. "Want me to help you look?"

"Maybe at some point, but he'll probably come back on his own."

"I think we can stay for a few minutes," Celeste said. "I'd like to meet your family."

They got out of the truck and walked across the field to where Manuel's relatives had gathered. Manuel introduced them to everyone. Manuel's dad, Enrique, was stocky and strong. Colton noticed his two chipped front teeth when he smiled big and tipped his hat to Celeste, with his eyes twinkling.

Yeah. He'd spent some time on horseback, okay. Colton knew a cowboy when he saw one.

There was a pink birthday cake on the picnic table nearby. A woman smiled and spoke to Manuel in Spanish. "It's her birthday. She wants you to stay for the cake," Manuel told them.

Just then, a soccer ball sailed through the air. One of Manuel's teenage cousins jumped, but it was way over his head. It plopped into the cake, bounced, then rolled onto the ground.

There was a discussion in Spanish.

"He'll go to Safeway and get another one," Manuel explained.

Colton gave Manuel the soccer papers, along with a key chain, and Manuel put them in a colorful woven plastic satchel by the picnic table.

Soon the cousin was back at the park, balancing a big pink box on the handlebars of a bicycle. Everyone happily sang a birthday song and ate cake from paper plates.

Colton joined in the soccer game for a little while. Celeste sat at the picnic table. When it was time to leave, Enrique and Uncle Alberto encouraged Colton to come every weekend and play.

When they got into the truck, Colton had a sinking feeling. Maybe Smoke was lying injured somewhere—or trapped—while Colton was learning how to kick a soccer ball through somebody's legs and run around and get it, and take it down the field.

Which, he had to admit, was a pretty good trick.

As soon as they got home, he called for Smoke some more.

No luck.

At dinner, Colton didn't eat much ravioli: it was yellow inside. More California cuisine.

He helped with the dishes and went back outside. There was a flock of wild turkeys pecking in the field by the windmill. The male opened his tail and puffed out the feathers on his chest; sunlight lit the white tips of his tail feathers from behind. He danced about, gobbling.

One by one, the turkeys flapped their wings and hopped up onto the roof of the shed, then awkwardly flew to the lowest branch of a eucalyptus tree and roosted in a row. The last one barely made it, flopping its wings and bonking the metal roof with bark and eucalyptus seed pods as it settled in for the night.

Wild turkeys: the world's most ungraceful birds, if they even qualified as birds.

What were more ridiculous: peacocks or wild turkeys? That would be a close call.

Colton sat on a rock in the field as the sun sank below the mountain. He imagined Smoke bounding toward him through the grass: a happy ending, like in a movie.

It was dark by seven. Inside, he and Celeste went on the Internet, searching under "Lost pets, Kingston County." They checked all the Web sites that had animals listed: both lost and found. "Guess we'll have to sit tight," Celeste told him. "Some of the shelters are closed on weekends; maybe someone will bring him in on Monday." She moved her chair back from the computer. "Want to look for good cougar Web sites? Work on your report, it'll keep your mind off Smoke."

"Okay."

Colton searched Yahoo! Kids for "cougar" and followed links to a Web site where he could print out a color brochure. He folded it so the image of the cougar was on the front. He stared at the cat's pink nose and the black tips of its ears. Under the picture it said: "The eyes of a fully grown mountain lion are sometimes grayish brown but often are a shimmering golden color."

Colton stared into its eyes. They looked like Smoke's.

He'll come back, Colton told himself.

But would he?

"Do you really think Smoke will come back?" Colton asked Celeste.

"He's only been gone a day," his mother answered, but that wasn't the answer Colton wanted to hear.

He opened the brochure and read: "You may be attracting mountain lions to your property without knowing it!"

There was a map of California and a pink rectangle for the key. Colton continued reading: "Mountain lions can be found where deer, their primary prey, are found."

A picture showed a mama lion and her kits. Below, it said: "They are specially protected mammals in California and cannot be hunted."

Good.

Not that Colton would want one to spring on the back of his neck from behind.

Which is how mountain lions attack, according to what Manuel had told him. The brochure emphasized that cougar attacks on humans are very, very rare.

Still, it advised people in cougar territory not to hike, bike, or jog alone. To stay in at dusk and dawn and at night. To keep a close watch on small children. Boy! You better believe that! Colton thought. Do not approach a mountain lion. If you encounter a mountain lion, do not run; instead, stand your ground. Face the animal, make noise, and try to look bigger by waving your arms; throw rocks or other objects. Pick up small children. If attacked, fight back.

Yikes.

Colton studied the photo of two footprints. It showed how a mountain lion track is different from a dog's track: no toenail prints. And a mountain lion track has an M-shaped pad. Colton slowly and carefully read the other information. "Mountain lions prefer deer, but, if allowed, they also eat pets and livestock."

"Mom?"

"Yes?"

"There aren't cougars around here, are there?"

"No. Not here. Maybe in the wilder ranges out by the coast, where it's less populated. We could talk to Angelo if you think we should be concerned. He's lived here all his life."

Gosh. Like that made him the world authority on everything?

"That's okay, Mom," said Colton. "I'm sure you're right."

Colton was tired. He went to bed, but he didn't want to go to sleep. He was afraid that Smoke would still be gone when he woke up. When he did sleep, he had a sad dream:

He was standing on the rocks above the spring. He noticed Angelo below, carrying something heavy wrapped in a towel. Colton knew it was Smoke. Angelo set him down in the grass and began to dig by the old corral, near the spring. There were calla lilies blooming, and Celeste was cutting them. Colton watched her cut all the calla lilies that were in bloom, all of them. She put them in Colton's arms. Colton slowly carried them to where there was a brown square cut into the ground. He put the lilies on the dirt. Then he began to drop Smoke's toy mice in with the flowers; as each one fell, it turned into a bird and flew away. His mother reached her hand out to him. "Why did Smoke go?" he asked.

Celeste didn't answer.

Colton awoke, his heart pounding.

He waited and worried all day Sunday. On Sunday evening, he and Celeste went to the back of the property and called and called again. They stood in the field, with wind swirling in the grass. "He's probably already dead, Mom," said Colton suddenly.

"Don't say that! He may have just gone off someplace . . ."

"Why would Smoke go off someplace?" Colton asked.

"Because he is a cat."

"He shouldn't have been outside yet. He doesn't know his way around. He's not used to California." Colton booted a rock. "He's from Idaho Falls."

Celeste put her arm around his shoulder, and they headed home.

In the porch light, they could see a basket lined with a red and white checkered cloth. A loaf of bread was in it, along with a bottle of LaRocca olive oil, some dark vinegar, and some bundles of rosemary, sage, and thyme.

"How thoughtful," said Colton's mom. "Wasn't that nice of Angelo?"

Colton didn't care about olive oil and herbs.

He didn't care about baskets of bread.

He wished Angelo would stay home.

Seven

Colton sat in his own seat on the bus Monday morning. "What's up, Colt?" Madison asked.

"Nothing."

"Tell the truth."

"Smoke ran away."

"He *did*? Did you call the shelter?"

"Yup. And checked on the Internet. My mom put up flyers."

Madison moved into the seat with Colton, put her hand on his arm, and patted it. "Well, I'll cross my fingers for you."

He looked over at her hand. His heart skipped a beat or two.

"I bet he'll come back. Maybe he fell in love with a girl

cat," she said quietly. "Maybe they ran off together for a while."

I doubt it, since he was neutered, Colton thought. But he wouldn't have said that out loud, not to Madison.

"You never know, Colt."

It was true. Anything was possible. At least talking to Madison made Colton feel that way. For the length of a bus ride, anyhow.

When she got off, his heart sank back down.

As he crossed the yard to his classroom, he heard Manuel shout his name. "Did you find your cat?"

"Not yet."

The bell rang.

After the morning's announcements and the Pledge, Mr. Viramontes pulled a small chair close to Colton's desk and sat down. "How's it going?"

Colton looked at his work sheet. "Fine."

"Your mom e-mailed me about your cat."

Colton frowned. She *did*?

"Shall we make some flyers in the computer lab?"

"She made some. Today she and the neighbor are putting them on telephone poles. She's putting an ad in *The Press Democrat*. And she's going by the shelter."

"Good."

"The neighbor walked up and down the road." Colton looked up at Mr. Viramontes. "At least he wasn't in the ditch."

"Yes," said Mr. Viramontes. "Thank God for that." He

stood up. "Well, if you want to write in your journal, that's fine by me. You don't have to finish those math problems unless you want to."

Colton did want to finish the math problems. After he checked every answer, he opened his journal. He stared out into space. Monique asked him: "You okay?"

And Colton said yes.

But a few minutes later Monique went up to Mr. Viramontes and whispered, "Something's wrong with Colton."

"Yes, I know. Thank you. And, Monique? I like how you look out for everybody."

Mr. Viramontes walked over to the Student of the Month display and looked at the picture of Smoke for a long moment. "Troublesome news," he told the class. "Colton's cat here disappeared in the middle of the night over the weekend. So Colton's worried."

Oh, great. Now everybody knew.

The class grew quiet.

"Maybe he got hit on the road," said Jared.

"No, don't say that!" cried Monique.

"Maybe a barn owl got him. Or a golden eagle!" said Jared. "My dad and I have seen eagles up on Kingston Mountain. Once we saw one in a field eating a jackrabbit. Once we saw a coyote run across the road!"

"Jared?" said Mr. Viramontes. "Let's not go there. I doubt an eagle could carry off a twenty-pound Maine coon cat."

"Maybe he's up a tree then," said Jared quietly.

"Much more likely," said Mr. Viramontes.

"Well, anyway, you're not supposed to let cats out at night," Jared added.

"Okay, Jared. That's enough," said Mr. Viramontes.

Liliana changed the subject. "Let's make some flyers in the computer lab!"

Colton sat with his elbow on his desk and his chin propped up with his hand. "We put up flyers already."

"In Spanish?" asked Daniela.

Actually, Colton hadn't thought of that.

"Great idea. Who will translate?" Mr. Viramontes asked.

Liliana and Daniela raised their hands. "We will!"

Colton gave the girls a careful description of Smoke—thick, black fur, yellow eyes, one white whisker—along with his mom's cell phone number.

The bell rang. Manuel picked up his soccer ball and walked out with Colton into the bright sunshine. They practiced trapping and passing the ball to each other. Jared raced over. "I'm playing! There's no closed games at Arroyo Elementary!"

Some other kids joined in, and soon a group of boys and girls were moving around on the field together like a school of fish.

Back inside, during silent reading, Colton stared at the words in his book but didn't read them. He thought about how Smoke cooled off in the sink in the bathroom like a big fat black caterpillar, his back to the world and his ears poking up—two black triangles with hairs at the tips.

How Smoke tossed and caught his toy mice, and dropped them into his food dish.

Where was he? Gone—like a puff of black smoke that disappeared into thin air.

Colton felt guilty. He'd let Smoke out and cats weren't safe out in the night, not where there were predators.

Jared was right about that.

At lunch, there was a hollow place in Colton's stomach that food couldn't fill. He peered into his sandwich and threw it away. He practiced soccer with Manuel. They didn't talk, just dribbled and passed to each other. Monique came out and found Colton. "Liliana and Daniela need you in the computer lab. Hurry up."

Colton and Manuel went through the back door into the computer lab. Colton could see Ms. Jensen through the glass divider, sitting behind the librarian's desk.

Good.

He looked at the computer screen. The girls were designing a flyer:

PERDIDO: KINGSTON MOUNTAIN ROAD
UN GATO NEGRO: "SMOKE"
GRANDE
OJOS AMARILLOS
UN BIGOTE BLANCO
NÚMERO DE TELÉFONO: 555-0915

"What font do you like?" Daniela asked him. She scrolled down the list. Colton picked one with a Western style.

Liliana changed the font, then pressed Command 2.

"Next we need a picture." A box came up. She typed in "cat," then clicked on Search.

"Which cat?" she asked.

Colton looked at the choices. "That one."

Liliana went to work with the tools, blackening and plumping up the cat, and making it furry. And making one whisker white. "Okay?"

"Okay," said Colton.

Manuel said to the girls, "I wish I could do that."

"We'll show you how to do it if you draw us each a puma," Liliana told him.

"Okay."

"And one for me, too," said Monique. "Colton, you draw it."

"Okay."

They printed out the flyer and went into the library.

Ms. Jensen looked up.

"Howdy," said Colton. "How are you doing?"

"I still have a little laryngitis!" she croaked, resting her hand on her throat.

"Can you please make copies for us?" Monique asked. "Twenty."

Ms. Jensen read the flyer. "What? Smoke is lost?" she said.

"We've searched everywhere."

The kids watched the sheets drop into the tray. "Well, if there's anything I can do to help, just let me know. Tell your mom."

"Thanks," Colton said.

"I'm going to ask my aunt to put one up in church," Liliana announced.

"And one at the community center," said Daniela.

"And, Manuel?" said Monique. "Ask your uncle to put one up in the restaurant." She gave him two flyers. "And put one at the duck park. Ms. Jensen? One for the library."

Colton didn't care if Monique gave a lot of orders; she was organized.

Jared walked in. "Why's everybody around here whispering?"

"It's a library," Monique told him.

"Can I use a computer?" Jared asked.

"No!" said Monique. "Time is up."

"She's right. Lunch is almost over," whispered Ms. Jensen.

Jared pointed to his ear. "I can't hear you!"

"That's because she lost her voice," said Monique.

"Then she should stay home!" Jared told Monique.

"You should stay home!" Monique told him. "Find a good place to put up one of these." She gave Jared a flyer. She and the other two girls marched out.

"Ms. Jensen. *What* is the point of trying to communicate . . . when nobody can hear you?" Jared asked.

Ms. Jensen frowned at him. "This is a library, so who cares if I whisper!"

"If you force your voice when you have laryngitis, you can injure your vocal cords," Jared told her. "Talk less, and you'll get your voice back sooner. Besides, what if you were needed suddenly to yell out emergency instructions. Like if there was an earthquake or something, and you had to evacuate the library. Then what? Huh?"

"Then I'll h-i-s-s-s-s-s-s-s-s! Like a Komodo dragon." Ms. Jensen took out a piece of paper and wrote: "Scram." She waved him out the door.

She looked at Colton after the others had left. "A bit immature," she whispered. "But not a bad kid." She peered at Colton over the top of her glasses. "You doing okay, my friend? I know what it's like to be missing a pet."

Colton asked, "Do you think he'll come back?"

"I hope so."

But she didn't say: I think so. Ms. Jensen always kept it real.

"My calico once got cooped up inside the frame of my Hide-a-Bed for three days," she whispered. "Late one night, I was reading and I heard a little muffled meow. I opened up the couch, and out she popped. A little scruffy looking, but basically okay."

"She was in a Hide-a-Bed?" whispered Colton.

"Yes! So keep your hopes up. Cats are crazy critters."

Back at class, Colton opened his journal. He turned to a new page and started writing. "My dad gave Smoke to me when I was two. I don't remember when he brought him home, but I wish I did. My dad named him Smoke, after a champion bucking bull." He closed his journal. Then he opened it up again and wrote, "If Smoke doesn't come back, I will never get another cat." He put the journal in the bottom of his desk, under all his books and notebooks.

At the end of the day, Monique gave Colton a folded paper with a rose and a heart drawn on the front with colored pens. Across it, inside the shape of an unfurling ribbon, was written: "Smoke."

All the kids in the class had signed it.

Jared wrote: "Get another cat. From Jared."

Colton was quiet on the bus ride home. When he was almost to his stop, he showed Madison the flyer. She agreed it was awesome. He translated the words for her. She asked if she could have one to put up in her school.

"Sure. Thanks." Colton gave a flyer to Madison. He said bye, got off the bus, and headed up the driveway with his mom.

"How was your day?"

"Fine." A lie, but so what. He didn't have to tell his mother everything.

Soccer practice was at Waldo School, from four to six o'clock. Celeste drove him down to the field. Manuel was already there. "Should I stay?" she asked.

"No thanks, Mom."

"You don't want me to sit in the bleachers?"

"No, that's okay, Mom. Just come back at six."

"But I would enjoy watching."

Colton looked at her.

"Fine. See you later," she said.

Dino introduced Colton and Manuel to the other kids and explained that each practice began with everyone sitting down and briefly checking in. The kids took turns talking about how they were doing while putting on socks, shin guards, and soccer cleats. Dino asked Colton and Manuel how their week went.

They said good. But that couldn't have been farther from the truth, on Colton's part. So far, it was the worst week of his life. At least within the span of his memory.

Everybody stretched, then jogged around the field. After that, more stretching—this time with partners. Next, drills: ball juggling and dribbling. Then, shots on the goalkeeper. It was intense. Manuel was the best player; no surprise there.

When they took a break, Dino walked over to Colton. "Good job," he said, and handed Colton a cup of Gatorade.

Colton took a drink.

Dino crossed his arms on his chest and looked at the ground. "Your mom e-mailed me and told me about your cat." He drew in the dirt with his shoe. "You okay?"

Colton said, "Yeah."

His mom e-mailed his soccer coach about his cat? Why not put it on the ten o'clock news!

"Once I had a cat named Bella. She was gone for a week. I thought she was gone for good. I was sitting on my deck and heard a little tiny meow, barely heard it. I couldn't tell where it was coming from at first. It was as if the wind was blowing her meow around. It sounded like it was coming from about ten different places.

"I got out my binoculars and scanned all the treetops, and there she was—up a pine. I swear I must have looked into that tree fifty times! But there she was. She had made it down to the lowest branch, but all the branches below it had been sawed off. So she was still about twenty feet above the ground.

"The building supervisor had an extension ladder, and we got her.

"Course I was busted because I wasn't supposed to have pets in the apartment. She lives with my parents now in Palm Desert. She's sweet sixteen. They just had a party. They all wore party hats. Bella, too. I've got pictures to prove it."

Dino bopped Colton on the shoulder. "Okay, then. Let's play ball."

After practice, Celeste said, "When's the next Soccer Time?"

Colton shrugged. "Not sure."

"Maybe sometime you could invite Angelo to play in a scrimmage. He was once on a rugby team. In Florence, Italy."

"Rugby is a lot different from soccer, Mom," Colton told her.

"What I'm saying is: I think he'd like to."

"Rugby's brutal, compared to soccer."

"I think he'd like to be more a part of your life—and mine. Most of his family is back east. He's never had a daughter or a son."

That was Angelo's problem—not his. Colton already had a dad.

Didn't Angelo realize that? Colton had a dad. Who Colton wanted to be more a part of his life.

Not that his mom did much to help make that happen.

Eight

Smoke was gone.

The birds sang quietly.

The sun didn't shine brightly over the barns; the sky was empty.

The air was thick and still.

At night the moon was dull and the stars were far away.

When Colton looked up at the sky, he thought about what his grandpa had said that last night they were together—about the cathedral. But he didn't feel like he was in it. The first evening star wasn't about luck, it was about being alone. The rock rolling in space felt lonely, empty. Colton missed his grandpa, and he was afraid he'd never see him again.

California wasn't all that great, not really. And now

Smoke had run off. Sure school was good and soccer was fun, but he wasn't good at soccer. He was mad his mom had dragged him away from Idaho Falls.

"E-mail Dino and say I quit," he told her.

"Quit?"

"Baseball's my game, Mom, in case you haven't noticed."

"E-mail him yourself. I'm not your personal secretary."

Whoa! Calm down, lady, Colton thought. But you better believe he didn't say that out loud.

"But before you do," she added, "you better stop to think it through. What about Manuel and the rest of the team? You and Manuel, you went into this together. Or have you forgotten?" She paused. "And what about Dino? Making a place for the two of you. Think he had to do that?

"He's a great guy. A great coach. Such passion for the game! What about Mr. Viramontes? Making an effort to find a team for you like he did. Going the extra mile for you."

She had a point there.

"Look, Colton. Do you think I'm not worried about Smoke? Think I don't miss him? I do! But people are depending on you. Don't let them down."

Have a hissy fit, lady, Colton said to himself.

He knew he wasn't really going to quit.

He'd just said it to make her mad.

An envelope arrived in the mail addressed to Colton. He opened it. Inside was a note card with "Francis Wells Mason" printed on the front. Inside, it said:

Dear Colton, The world is full of wonderful people. Maybe one of them is caring for Smoke, somewhere—and that person will eventually locate you. If Smoke has departed this earth, look for his spirit: it will be around you, in the sunlight, where it rests like gold in the grass and shimmers in the leaves of the trees. If he is gone, be comforted knowing that he was a very lucky cat to have had such a great boy as you. You loved him. He loved you back. Sincerely, Frank

The note didn't make Colton feel better, not really.

When Smoke left, it seemed like a shadow was cast over Colton—a big shadow, bigger than the shadow of a cat. Where had he gone? He'd walked out. And left nothing behind but empty space, a space bigger than the cat that had filled it. And darker. A space darker and deeper and emptier than a canyon.

At school Colton did his work, finished his math problems, worked on his wildlife report, but he felt numb.

At school on Thursday, he stared at his journal.

Jared looked over at Colton, then raised his hand. "Mr. Viramontes? Guess what. Yesterday I saw a woman from Animal Rescue with six kittens outside of Pet Stop. Colton should get another cat."

"I don't want another cat," said Colton quietly.

"Anybody who takes a kitten from Animal Rescue gets a free starter kit: a bag of kibbles, a bag of Tidy Kitty, and a rubber rat with a bell on its tail. All the kittens have been checked out by the vet and already have their first set of shots. And have also been wormed. But it's adults only," continued Jared. "And she interviews the family, so bring your mom and dad."

Monique stared at Jared. "Did you hear him? He doesn't want a kitten from Pet Stop!"

"Sorry, but he should try harder to feel better. You're responsible for your own happiness."

"Jared? Please. Nobody wants Colton to feel bad," said Mr. Viramontes. "But feeling better may not be a matter of just getting another cat." He paused. "In fact, I've never gotten another dog since I lost my dog, Luke. Four years ago. Although I've often thought about it."

"No offense, but I think you should get over it," said Jared. "There are so many puppies out there that need a good home! Think about it. You need to move on!"

Mr. Viramontes ignored Jared. "Lukie and I were connected—two beings on a planet." He paused. "He was a dazzling spirit who experienced the world as a dog. Bless Lukie's heart, he was my friend. See? It chokes me up. Even now." He lifted his glasses and mopped the corners of his eyes with his handkerchief. "What can I tell you? I loved my dog."

He blew his nose.

Colton's heart felt heavy for Mr. Viramontes. And for Lukie. But he had to remind himself, Smoke might still come home. He might! Smoke wasn't in the past, not yet.

He wasn't! Don't give up on him, he told himself. He's out there someplace!

"Your father called to check in," Celeste told Colton when he got off the bus. "Finally."

"Where's he at?"

"Idaho someplace."

"Did you tell him about Smoke?" Colton asked.

"Yes. He said to tell you he knew a rodeo clown who lost a cat and it showed up a month later."

"A month?"

Celeste shrugged her shoulders.

"Supposedly. But, Colton?" She paused. "You know, for every story with a happy ending, there's also one . . ."

"I know, Mom." Colton began to walk ahead of Celeste. Then he suddenly turned and said, "You never have anything good to say about Dad."

"What do you want me to say?"

"Anything!"

"I told you the bear story."

"What was good about that?"

"Okay. He's a good tipper."

"I'm serious, Mom!"

"I am, too. He's generous, a good provider. He always pays child support and chips in on the other things."

"What else?"

"He's fearless."

Colton looked at her.

Actually his grandpa had told him his dad was afraid of spiders—certain ones, anyway.

Celeste said, "You think I've never seen him ride a bull? He defines the term 'rodeo star.' Right?"

"Yeah."

"But bull riding is reckless—"

"In your opinion, not everyone's," Colton said. "It's dangerous, yeah. Not everybody thinks it's 'reckless.' "

"Yes, everybody does! And anyway, he doesn't know when to quit." She paused. "But without him, I wouldn't have you. So, no regrets."

He'd heard that before. Still, it was good to hear it again.

"It didn't help that what's-her-name, the rodeo queen, rode into his life," she added, "just when I was thinking we might have a chance to get back together again. But c'est la vie, it's over. It's been over. It's time for me to move on, and I have."

"Her name is Cheryl, Mom."

Colton didn't even believe he said that out loud.

But now that he'd said it, he'd finish: "And, Mom? If you end up wanting to stay here in California, and I don't, then I've been wondering—what if I headed on back to Idaho and lived with Dad and Cheryl?"

"Live where with them? Where? In an RV?"

Colton didn't answer.

"What would you do about school?"

"Maybe live with Grandpa, then. Go to the junior high. There's a junior high! Then, I could go to the high school—

that brick high school Dad and Uncle Chad went to. Play baseball."

"You mean the one they dropped out of?"

"Yeah."

"You think you'd like to live at the end of two ruts in a meadow ten miles outside of nowhere? What kind of life would that be for you, Colton?"

"I would be okay with it. When I got my license, I could work at the Wagon Wheel, bus dishes."

"That's two and a half hours away."

"Get me an old truck and fix it up. Work at the Wagon Wheel on weekends. Go to school. Grandpa needs somebody to lend him a hand around the place."

Celeste stared at him. "Well, what about his sons? Shouldn't his sons be the ones worrying about that?"

"Grandpa's limp is getting worse—he has arthritis in that hip and—"

Colton stopped talking. He bit his bottom lip. Hard.

"And last summer, he almost fell crossing the South Fork, Mom. He barely made it. I'm afraid he might get swept away or hurt somehow and die out on that ranch alone."

"Wes is a tough old bird."

"Not anymore he isn't."

"Well, in any event, decisions like these are complicated. That's why they're not made by kids. I'm sorry, Colton. Whether you live with me or Dad or Wes, it's just not your call."

Colton stared at her.

"But I do understand how you feel about Wes. He's a wonderful man. Maybe we can reevaluate the situation at some point in the future. Look at it again, under whatever new circumstances we might be in."

"When, Mom?"

"I don't know when. But not when you're twelve, or thirteen, that's for sure."

"What about when I'm fourteen, or fifteen?"

"Maybe then, but let's just give California a chance, see how things unfold."

"Okay, but I'm planning to go to ranching school and help Grandpa with the ranch when I'm grown."

"Ranching school? I thought you wanted to be a wildlife illustrator. Or photographer."

"I'm not sure now. Louise's been telling me about a ranching college out in Montana."

"Fine. But that's years from now, Colton. Let's focus on the present."

The next day, Colton wrote in his journal: "Out here, I'm a long way from home. I miss Idaho, and I can't wait till the end of December to see my grandpa. I want to see my dad ride in a rodeo." He decided not to write in the journal about Cheryl. That she was a trick-riding rodeo star with her own Web site. And that he'd love to see her ride, too! He missed Cheryl. Even though he hadn't actually spent that much time around her. He was glad his dad and Cheryl got engaged last year, although he didn't think his mom knew that yet. And would probably be mad when she found out.

But maybe he'd tell Madison about Cheryl. That Cheryl had a classic '66 Corvette ragtop. Why shouldn't he? Cheryl would be his stepmom someday soon.

Maybe he'd show Madison the horseback picture. Not like she'd judge his dad by his teeth. They were fixed now—he had a whole mouthful of new white ones. Too white, actually; the dentist went overboard.

He left the journal on Mr. Viramontes's desk.

It made him feel better to write about missing Idaho, his dad, his grandpa.

End of December, he'd be at the ranch. It would be cold; the ground would be frozen and dusted with snow. But they'd build a fire in the woodstove in the kitchen and sit around and tell stories. That was Colton's favorite.

End of December, Colton would split kindling off a pine board with a hatchet like his grandpa showed him; he'd build another one-match fire without any paper, under the watchful eye of his grandpa.

When the chimney needed cleaning, they'd let the fire go out. They'd pull the chimney off in sections and take it outside, and bang and bang it till the creosote fell onto the snow. His grandpa banging on that chimney in the quiet of the ranch was the loudest noise Colton ever heard in his life.

Since it would be around the holidays, maybe Grandpa would tell Colton the ghost story—the one about the quiet, creepy rap-rap-rapping sound in the dark woods that turns out to be a box of wrapping paper.

Maybe he'd scare his mom with that one when it got closer to the holidays. She knew it, but if he timed it right, she'd scream when he jumped at her.

End of December, maybe Smoke would be back.

Boy, I hope so, Colton thought.

But what if he wasn't?

Colton just tried not to go there.

Being at school was still hard. Mr. Viramontes told the boys it was time to do something besides draw for the report. Although their drawings were awesome. So they read about cougars in English and Spanish, took notes and wrote down page numbers, then rephrased the information so it wouldn't be cheating. The bibliography was the worst, getting all the commas and periods in the right places. Colton hated the nit-picking small stuff, but at least Manuel was in it with him.

And Colton had the bus ride home to look forward to. So he focused on that.

He tried to hide from Madison that he was down in the dumps, but she saw right through it. He appreciated that she didn't ask him questions. He liked just sitting nearby and saying nothing.

Madison handed him a card in an envelope as he got up to get off the bus.

Colton slid it into his back pocket, then walked up to the house with Celeste. Charcoal clouds were gathering against a background of bright blue; one or two raindrops hit Colton.

Celeste said, "There's an Italian film festival over in Kingston. Angelo and I are going to see an Italian Western. First we're having dinner. We'd absolutely love it if you would join us."

In other words: Go on a date with Celeste and Angelo.

"No thanks, Mom."

Colton didn't stop at the fridge for a snack. He went straight up to his room. He closed the door and took the envelope out of his pocket. On the front was a picture of a campfire with a bunch of cowpokes standing around it. Smoke was rising up to the night sky—full of stars. Inside, Madison had written:

Dear Colt, I'm sorry Smoke is still missing. I hold good thoughts for him, and you. I just want you to know that I feel sad. Love, Maddie.

With a daisy over the *i*.

Tears sprang into Colton's eyes. You cry and you're worthless, he told himself. Get a hold of yourself.

Colton lay on his bed with the card on his chest and looked up. He just lay there, feeling so bad about Smoke it made his chest ache and his stomach sick.

Smoke was gone, and probably forever. You should have kept him in a while longer, till he knew the ropes.

You could have walked him with the harness till he got used to the place.

No he shouldn't have! A cat on a leash—that was where Colton drew the line.

When he opened the envelope to slide Madison's card back in, he saw a small, folded paper. He opened it:

For Colt
by Maddie

The Long Way Home

When you hope
he makes it through,
other hearts
are hoping, too.

When you call him
home to you,
other voices
call him, too.

Hearts and cats
that love to roam
sometimes take
the long way home.

"Colton?"
"Up here!"

Colton hid the card and the poem under his pillow and sat up as his mom came up the stairs.

"Are you okay?"

"Yeah. Why?"

"Just asking."

"I'm fine."

"Well, are you comfortable staying alone? We won't be back till about midnight."

"Yes, Mom. I'm fine."

"Elmo and the heelers can stay with you if you want."

"No thanks, I don't need dogs to babysit me. I'm fine!"

"Okay, well, I guess I'll get ready then. Angelo's coming at five. There are some interesting leftovers in the fridge."

"Okay, thanks."

"Prosciutto, wrapped in white paper."

No thanks, Colton thought. "Okay, Mom, thanks."

Celeste went back downstairs, and Colton took out Maddie's poem and read it, over and over again. He checked out the cowboy card again, too. "Love, Maddie"? That had to make him feel a little better, anyway. And it did.

In fact, Colton began to get a feeling—a strong feeling—that Smoke was still alive.

Taking the long way home.

That he was shut in somewhere, where he couldn't get out.

But where? thought Colton. Where?

They'd looked in the barns and outbuildings, opened up

the door of the tack room. Sure, Smoke could survive on bugs for a while. But he'd already been lost out there for a week!

Then Colton had a thought: What if Angelo missed seeing Smoke in the dark—in the old cabin, up by the spring? There wasn't any electricity up there anymore. Angelo probably couldn't see diddly-squat. Maybe Angelo had scared Smoke—with his dogs. Maybe Smoke had stayed hidden in the shadows of the cabin; black against black would be hard to see. Behind the woodstove. Just two yellow eyes.

But how could Smoke get in there? That cabin was locked!

The windows were boarded up!

Still, there could be a way in, somehow. And not out. Through the chimney, maybe—now that was a thought.

Or maybe he'd gotten shut in that stone pump house. Maybe Angelo had checked—not seen Smoke in the dark, eating spiders. Behind the donkey engine. And then closed the door and shut him in. Now that was a possibility.

Colton heard the shower running downstairs. He heard the water shut off, then the hair dryer blasting. What if Smoke had fallen down the well!

There's a lid on it, he told himself.

With a six-inch hole that Angelo hasn't bothered to fix yet?

Be rational. Smoke would not be stupid enough to fall into a hole.

Probably.

Unless he was lured in by delicious crickets creeping around on the walls.

And potato bugs!

Colton went downstairs. He found an open box of Ritz crackers in the cupboard and tucked it under his arm. He kicked off his shoes and sat in the living room. He turned on the TV.

After a while, Celeste walked in.

Whoa!

It had been a very, very long time since Colton had seen his mom in a dress and high-heeled shoes. "Sure you don't want to come?" she asked.

"Yup."

Celeste smelled like flowers. She picked up her jacket and purse. She stopped for a minute and put on some lipstick in the mirror. "If anything comes up, call Louise. Her number's by the phone."

"Okay."

"I have to turn my cell phone off in the movie. And in the restaurant. I'll put it on vibrate. And check for messages. Call if you need us."

"Okay, Mom!"

Celeste turned around and looked at him. "Well, I've been worried about you! You've gotten kind of distant, Colton. I know you're concerned about Smoke, and so am I. But are you doing okay—otherwise?"

There was a knock at the door. "You didn't have a snack when you came in."

Colton shook the box of crackers at her.

"Those are completely stale!

"Coming!" she called. She pointed one toe in Colton's direction and quietly asked, "What do you think of the shoes?"

"Better than the red clogs."

"Well, that's a start, I guess." She opened the door. Angelo walked in, stylish in a black shirt, black jacket, boots, and jeans. "Wow! You look just beautiful, Celeste!" he said.

"Thank you."

"Colton coming?"

Celeste said, "Unfortunately, no."

Angelo called in: "You sure, Colton? I think you'd like the film. It's a Western. There are subtitles but—"

"I'm sure. Thanks, though."

"And Cafe La Giostra got four stars in the paper. Good grub. Great rib eye steak, in fact."

"No, but thanks."

"Remember, stick around," Celeste told him. "Don't go wandering off anywhere."

"In the rain?"

"Well, I'm just saying: Don't wander off."

"I won't."

You're a liar, Colton told himself.

"And lock the door when it gets dark."

"I will."

"Remember, Louise's home if there's any problem."

"You already told me this, Mom."

"The number's by the phone. She's seven minutes away."

"Celeste?" said Angelo gently. "We'll only be gone for a few hours. We'll be back by midnight.

"Maybe twelve-thirty," he told Colton.

Colton said, "No rush."

Angelo helped Celeste with her coat. No point in telling them to bring Smoke back the leftovers in a kitty bag.

Colton stood at the window and watched as they crossed the gravel to Angelo's car—both under one umbrella, heads practically touching. Angelo opened the car door for her.

He closed the umbrella and got in on the other side.

Colton watched them head down the driveway and pull out onto the road.

Nine

Good. Colton was on his own. A perfect opportunity to check out the territory up by the cabin and the spring. For himself.

The cabin was close to home; the ranch was home.

For now, anyway.

He took the steps up to his room two at a time.

Sure, his mom would say that Angelo already checked the cabin. As if Mister Know-It-All couldn't make a mistake or something. And Angelo *was* a know-it-all, in his own way. Maybe he was even worse than Jared.

But Angelo didn't know everything, like his mom thought he did. The guy probably took his heelers up there to look. Now why would Smoke come out of hiding with four sneaky blue heelers sniffing around?

Well, Lily wasn't that sneaky, but the others were.

And why should he depend on Angelo, anyway?

Smoke wasn't Angelo's cat; Smoke was Colton's cat, and he'd had him since he was two. He was Colton's responsibility. And Colton needed to find him.

Now! Before it was too late. That was pretty basic, wasn't it? When someone or something is lost, get on out there and look for him till you find him. Rain or shine.

Colton opened his closet door and found his cowboy boots. He pulled them on and walked around the room. They were a little snug, but they basically fit.

A cowboy hat is about function, not style, Colton told himself. So what if the brim is bent? He put it on. Colton pulled his Carhartt jacket off a hanger. A little tight; so what? He caught a glimpse of himself in the mirror. He pushed the hat farther back on his head. That was more like it.

On his way out, Colton stopped at the computer and went to the Professional Rodeo Cowboys Association home page, then typed "Jesse Hudson" into the Search box. Up came his favorite picture of his dad—from back when he was the champion, first time around.

Talk about cowboys sitting around a campfire—he'd print that one out for Madison. Show her what a cowboy looked like on the back of a 2,500-pound bull!

He pressed Command P but didn't wait for the slow old printer to be done. He'd get it later. He had bigger fish to fry—finding Smoke.

It was wet out. Clouds were low and gray. Gusts of wind blew through branches as Colton followed a row of eucalyptus trees, with big sheets of bark peeling off their trunks. Shiny, curved brown leaves and hard seed pods were scattered on the ground. Colton loved the spicy scent of eucalyptus. Not as pretty as sage, but close.

He walked through the trees past the small old windmill, creaking and spinning slowly. He stopped to pull down on the brim of his hat and snap up his jacket.

It was then that he thought he heard a meow.

Where was it coming from?

Could have been anywhere. Wind was riling up the trees.

He jammed his hands into his pockets. You said you wouldn't wander off.

So what? he asked himself scornfully. And you're not wandering off, you're on a hunt for a lost pet, while your mother and her boyfriend cozy up in a booth and toast each other with red wine.

What if Smoke is down to his last meow?

It took a while to get up the slippery, grassy hill and into the trees. Longer than Colton thought it would. He continued through the woods. Raindrops hit the leaves above him. Out in the open, rain thumped on his hat.

He went up the rickety porch steps of the cabin, reached over the door for the key, and turned it in the lock under the old white porcelain doorknob.

He stepped into the room.

"Smoke?" he said.

There was a low, long roll of thunder.

Colton's fifth-grade teacher had warned the kids not to play in abandoned buildings. Was the cabin abandoned? Not technically. And he wasn't playing. But he got a creepy feeling—as if he were being watched. He heard a branch scratch against the outside wall, heard rain patter on the metal roof.

Colton didn't discount the ghost of Jackson Parker, not completely. If some old rancher guy was a ghost now, then so be it. You had to feel for anybody killed hunting. And it was sad about his wife up there alone, a young widow, dressed in black, digging his grave.

Still, Colton glanced over his shoulder, back through the doorway, past the porch. The little old apple trees were soaked. Rain was falling steadily; the sky was darkening.

A thin, striped mattress was on the iron bed; pack rats had pulled out the stuffing. A worn, dusty bedspread was falling onto the floor. Colton looked under the bed. "Smoke?"

The table was carpeted with dust, no cat prints. A worn, oval braided rug was underneath it. Rodents had been working on that, too.

Colton crossed the small room, checked behind the woodstove, and went into the kitchen. "Smoke? You in here, boy?"

He opened every cupboard: empty, except for faded flowered shelf paper, thumbtacked to the wood with rusty tacks. He turned on the faucet: no water. There was a galvanized bucket under the sink, and it was full of tools: two pipe wrenches, a big hammer with a broken claw, a chisel, a long, Phillips-head screwdriver with electrical tape on the handle. At the bottom, some big old rusty screws, bolts, and a few huge sixteen-penny nails. Seemed to Colton there was a bucket like that in every shed he'd ever been in.

"Smoke?"

One of the kitchen drawers was half open. He saw an ice pick, a fork. A rubber stopper, an oily red mechanic's rag, shredded—maybe a mouse nest. Or rat.

Colton reached for an aluminum film container and unscrewed the lid. Just what he suspected: mice-proof wooden matches. Matches in a film container, something his grandpa would do. Colton screwed the lid back on and tossed it back into the drawer.

He closed and locked the cabin and hung up the skeleton key. Rain was falling, heavier now. He turned up his collar in the back. He checked the pump house behind the donkey engine and saw a black spider with long, pointy legs hanging upside down in a web. Maybe Smoke had been bitten by a black widow!

Through all that fur?

Let me out of here, Colton told himself, even though he knew black widows pretty much stick to hanging in their webs, not jumping out at somebody.

Colton located the hand-dug well. He got down on his knees in the wet grass and looked in. He wished he had a flashlight. He dropped a pebble and listened for the splash. "Smokey?" he called. "You down there, boy?"

Of course not! How could a twenty-pound cat fit through a six-inch opening? You're stupider than Angelo, Colton told himself. Shut up and get real.

He continued on to the spring. There was a lot of wildlife up by that spring; maybe something had treed Smoke in one of the tall cypresses. It was hard to see up there; the branches were so thick and dark. The needles were so dense. Sure, sure, Angelo already allegedly checked the trees. But it wasn't like Smoke would have wanted to be found hiding in the tallest branches—with four dogs staring up at him from below.

Maybe not Lily, but the other three would have been.

Besides, Dino's cat had been up a tree he probably looked in fifty times!

As he neared the spring, Colton noticed some cattle in the distance. It caught his eye—how they were moving, as if keeping their distance from something.

But what? He continued to watch. Why were they staying in a group? Not running, just walking away. Together.

Why?

An odd feeling crept over Colton, and the voice in his head said, "Get out of here. Leave."

Colton searched the grassy, rocky hillside. He noticed an animal slinking slowly up the hill, tan, belly close to the ground. Stretched out, it seemed to be about six or eight feet long. Was it a deer?

Colton watched it.

Of course it wasn't a deer! A deer didn't slink; it walked, or ran.

Was it a dog or a coyote? Colton squinted to get a better look.

What was it—moving so low in the grass, with a long tail, and creeping like a cat?

It *was* a cat. A big one!

Colton felt his skin tingle on the back of his neck and his heart begin to race. Calm down, he told himself. Get a hold of yourself. He looked down. There, in the soft mud at the edge of the spring, he saw the perfect imprint of a huge paw. He stooped to get a closer look. Rain was pooling in it. He looked for claw marks. There were none. And at that moment he heard a loud, wailing scream from the hillside above him.

Stand up, he told himself. Stand up now. Face the hill. And don't run. Whatever you do, don't run.

Slowly, Colton retreated toward the cabin, backwards—hat in the air.

He heard a scream again, this time closer—unearthly, bloodcurdling. It sent a shudder through him.

It just shook him to the core.

He moved in slow motion up the cabin steps—fumbled for the skeleton key and unlocked the door. But his hands were trembling, and he dropped the key when he pulled it out of the keyhole; it fell between the cracks in the porch floor and landed out of reach in the dirt below.

Colton hurried into the cabin and shut the door behind him; but the latch on the old porcelain doorknob didn't catch, so the door just popped open again, and again, as he tried to close it. He locked it with the flimsy hook and eye that dangled from the doorjamb.

He stood there, his heart pounding.

He heard the rain hitting the metal roof and the wind blowing against the cabin walls. Stay calm. He remembered what his fifth-grade teacher said: If you're in danger, your first job is to make yourself safe.

Good old Mrs. Barron!

Colton dumped out the galvanized bucket and picked up the rusty hammer and sixteen-penny nails. He walked to the door and, with many loud blows, nailed it shut, striking the nail heads again and again, and sinking the nails through the door and deep into the doorjamb.

Yeah, he knew how to use a hammer. Thank you, Grandpa Wes!

And Dad.

He felt better, knowing he was nailed in.

He got up on the chair and peered through the crack between the boards covering the window. He couldn't see much: just the wind tossing black branches against the sky.

He pictured the cougar standing by the spring, turning its head and looking in his direction—the way he and Manuel had drawn it. With those yellow eyes, that steely gaze.

Colton and Manuel had read about how somebody

stabbed a cougar in the eyeball with a pen and survived an attack on a trail up in Oregon. Colton hated to think it, but he could stab the cougar in the eye with the ice pick—if he had to.

He went and got it from the kitchen drawer. He set it on the table. He heard another long, low rumble of thunder.

He sat down, back against the wall.

He was uncomfortable—damp, tired, and hungry. An hour passed, maybe more. He could barely see inside the cabin, barely make out the table, the woodstove.

This would be a long night, okay!

Colton stopped breathing.

What was that? Something was out there!

Along with the wind, he thought he heard the sounds of a whisper—a deep, faint, raspy whisper saying:

". . . C-o-o-o-o-o-o-l-d . . . c-o-o-o-o-o-l-d . . ."

There's no such thing as a ghost. It's the wind!

But he heard it again: "Co-o-o-o-ld . . . Where are you-u-u-u?" And the doorknob rattled!

A moment later he heard the pump house door creak.

Colton curled his fingers around the wooden handle of the ice pick and held it tight.

It isn't anything, he told himself. Nothing but the wind.

You're hearing things, boy.

Colton listened to himself breathe, to his own heart beating. Calm down!

Calm down. Let go of the ice pick.

Breathe.

Colton closed his eyes. He felt so tired. He sat with his eyes shut, listening to the rain gently falling.

He heard a thud on the roof and scrambled to his feet.

What was up there?

Above his head, he heard footsteps cross the roof.

He got down on his hands and knees and searched around in the dark for the nuts and bolts and nails he had dumped out on the floor. He threw them back into the galvanized bucket, then shook and rattled it.

He shook and rattled it some more.

Then he listened.

He pictured the face of the mountain lion: cold, wet, and hungry. He pictured it growling, hissing. Its ears flat—lips curled back, fangs gleaming. Was it still on the roof? Or had it dropped into the bushes to lie in wait under cover of darkness, its yellow eyes watching from between the black leaves . . .

He kept listening.

See?

It had worked.

He'd scared it off.

His dad hadn't thought making noise was important at French Camp, but he was wrong. If he had listened and had some pots to bang on, maybe he wouldn't have got the door ripped off his camper and got a bear drunk.

His mom was smart, and she was right.

Colton thought of her and Angelo at Cafe La Giostra,

eating fettuccine Alfredo. Mmm-mmm. Warm, creamy white pasta with fresh grated cheese. Nothing to complain about that.

Boy. He'd rethink that rib eye steak offer now.

He thought of his mom's lovely, fluffy blond curls and eyes as blue as blueberries. The same color as his. What would she think when she came home at twelve-thirty and discovered he was gone?

With luck, she wouldn't check his room.

Fat chance of that.

But Colton couldn't dwell on it. He had more pressing questions to answer.

Could a cougar rip boards off a window?

He knew the answer: A cougar could jump into a tree with a deer in its mouth.

So yes, a cougar could tear off a few boards with its claws.

He pulled out all of the kitchen drawers and pried them apart. The fronts of the drawers were the thickest. He nailed those across the corners of the windows from the inside.

You're safe, Colton told himself.

If you stay in here.

Not that you could ever get out.

Stay alert, he told himself. Don't sleep!

But what else was there to do? He sat on the edge of the bed, with the hammer beside him on the mattress and the bucket nearby on the floor. He snapped up his jacket, all the way to the neck. Then he tipped over. He pulled the dusty, thin white bedspread with the little white balls up over him.

Even with his jacket snapped, Colton felt cold. His boots and the bottoms of his jeans were wet. But he got as warm as he could under the flimsy cover.

He thought of the ghost of Jackson Parker, climbing up out of that hand-dug well. First his skinny fingers would be sliding the lid off, then you'd see the top of his hat, then the brim, bent up.

Then his face, with the swollen eyes. Just staring straight at you!

And his mouth, as dark and empty as the hole he just crawled out of.

Think of something else, Colton told himself. He thought of a better lookin' ghost: the ghost rider. With his silver saddle, sparkling in the light.

The empty glove, empty boots.

Skulls on them.

And crossbones.

Horse as black as night.

His eyes popped open.

What was that?

He thought he heard the distant sound of horses' hooves drumming on the ground.

You're so tired you can't think straight! Hungry, too.

Dang! He wished he hadn't thrown away his sandwich at lunch. Even though it was a turkey and pesto sandwich, with provolone cheese.

What ever happened to tuna sandwiches, anyway? Or PB&Js?

If he ever made it back alive, he'd make himself a couple of regular old sandwiches.

Still . . . what he wouldn't give for a warm loaf of Angelo's homemade bread, and some olive oil and dark vinegar to dunk it in.

He lay there in the dark.

Truth was, he was miserable.

Scared, too.

And lonely.

Don't cry! he told himself.

Be a man—you're twelve. Sink or swim.

You're responsible for yourself; nobody's going to take care of you. Nobody's going to help you out of this situation. You better grow up, boy.

He heard an owl hoot.

He heard another owl answer.

His mom would be home soon. She'd be so worried about him. Colton thought of making a run for it, out into the open, but no. Run all the way down in the dark? Never run when there's a cougar around, the brochure had said. Never walk, even—alone in the dark—with a cougar around.

Besides, the door was nailed shut.

Colton wished that half of the claw wasn't broken off the hammer.

When would it be light?

How many hours more before the sun came back up?

Many.

Think of Madison. He pictured her face—dimple on just that one side, dark, bright eyes, thick black lashes, and shiny brown hair. It made him feel calm, to think of Madison. This would work out. Make a plan for the morning, he told himself. In the morning, you can split the molding off around the door with the hammer and chisel. Then pop it off. This will work out.

When the sun's up high enough, and you can see what's out there, walk on down and catch heck from your mother.

Boy.

That was a thought! In fact, it was the one thought he had that made him wish the night would last a little longer.

Ten

Colton woke up, freezing.

How long had he slept? There was no way to know. A little moonlight was sliding through the crack between the boards. The rain had stopped. The owls had quit hooting. There was more light in the room. Maybe the sky had opened up; maybe the clouds had blown away.

He lay there shuddering, teeth chattering. You better warm up, boy, he told himself. Live or die. Well, maybe it wasn't live or die, but he was just chilled to the bone.

There's nobody here to warm you up; you're not ten. Six months and you'll be thirteen. There are matches in that film container. There's a woodstove.

What are you waiting for?

In the dim light, Colton fumbled for the chisel and one of

the thin, flat pine boards that had been on the back of a broken drawer. He positioned the chisel close to the edge of the board and struck the end with the hammer. A thin piece cracked and split off. He could barely see what he was doing. Cut your finger off and bleed to death, he told himself. That's all you need.

He worked carefully, splitting the drawer into long, thin spears of kindling. Soon he had a pile of them.

He collected tufts of cotton fiber that the mice had pulled from the mattress. He picked up the oily mechanic's rag. That ought to burn. He peeled the paper from the kitchen shelves and made a big sticky wad. And gathered up the rest of the slats.

He swung open the woodstove door. He constructed a pyramid of kindling and slats, small to big. With the cotton fiber, rag, and shelf paper underneath.

Sure Colton could build a one-match fire with no paper on a sandbar in the daytime with lots of dry sticks around.

Now all he had was four old matches.

Cross your fingers, he told himself.

Then he struck a match on the side of the stove. It didn't even spark, just snapped the crumbly tip off. Three left. Careful, boy. Colton struck a second match. He waited for the matchstick to burn brightly and carefully touched it to the shelf paper. Good. It lit, but barely, and began to smoke. Colton watched a thin blue line of fire burn along one edge. But the flame flickered and went out.

Colton could see that shelf paper wasn't going to help

him. He saved what was left of the two burned matchsticks. He struck the third match; when the flame was yellow and burning its way down the stick, he lit the other two matchsticks. Fire caught in the cotton and then in the thin sticks of wood. Good.

A one-match fire-building technique taught by Smokey Bear himself. Never mind that it took three; they were old. Colton gently blew the flame to life, but wait a minute.

How long had it been since the chimney was cleaned out?

About fifty years, you dope! Colton told himself. And you're nailed in here!

He broke the fire apart.

The flames went out; smoke rose up.

A scared, lonesome feeling came over Colton.

What if he froze?

What if he fell asleep and never woke up again?

What if he never saw anybody again?

This is California, the land of golden sunshine, not Idaho. It's not winter! It's fall.

Course you will.

Hang in there—it'll be morning soon.

But when?

Colton wasn't religious in the regular sense, but that didn't mean he counted out the possibility. So he said a prayer:

"Please walk with my grandpa when he crosses the river. Please cross with him to the other side. At least until I get him that trekking stick. And keep your eye on Dad, too, while you're at it. So he doesn't break his doggone neck.

Please help him see when it's time to quit. If he gets kicked any more in the head, he'll probably never know on his own.

"Please fly with Chad. And ride with Cheryl. Don't let her fall off her horse, because I can see from her Web site she rides like a wild woman.

"Please take care of my mom. Please don't let her come up here looking for me, please. Please don't let the cougar get her."

He thought he'd better add: "Or Angelo, either, for that matter.

"To be honest, I've never been to church, so I don't know if I qualify for requests.

"And I also know you've got more to worry about than one lost cat, considering the condition of the world.

"But if Smoke is dead, please let him stay with you. If he's alive, please bring him home. If he's out there lost, please help me find him. If that was him meowing, please tell him to shut up and stay put—till I get myself out of this mess.

"Please don't let the cougar get him. I know a cougar gets hungry, but Smoke's a good old boy.

"And by the way, if that cougar's asleep up on this roof or hiding in the bushes, I wouldn't mind if you told it to move on out of here.

"Okay, that's it then."

Colton lay there, thinking up words with jack to tell Celeste if she ever spoke to him again:

Jack-of-all-trades.

Was there a Jacksonville someplace? It seemed to him there was.

Flapjacks!

Yes to flapjacks!

He was so hungry. If he made it through the night, and when his mom cooled down, he'd ask if she'd make him a big stack of pancakes for breakfast. And not crepes! Pancakes —big, thick granddaddy ones. With melted butter on top and syrup spilling down and dripping over the edges.

It was just then—just when he was feeling a little better about his situation—that he heard it: the unmistakable sound of something big moving through the brush, fast and up close. It thumped the side of the wall and jumped onto the porch—with a thud. He heard a sudden wild, crazy scratching of claws, tearing at the bottom of the door!

Stand your ground, Colton told himself. Fight back!

Colton picked up the hammer. He slid between the woodstove chimney and the wall. He could see the white porcelain doorknob shaking and turning.

Make noise! he told himself. And he started banging on the chimney as loud and as hard as he could.

But the door split apart and slammed into the wall.

The hammer slid from Colton's hand onto the floor.

The silhouette of a tall, shadowy figure in a wide-brimmed hat filled the doorway—backlit by the moon.

From under the hat, two dark eyes were looking straight at him, one eye half shut. Cheek all swollen. Mouth partway open, just a black hole. Arm stretched out stiff and sleeve torn off, jacket shredded at the shoulder. Jeans dripping wet, pant leg hung up on the top of one boot.

And then Colton saw it: one white star, glowing in the dark.

"Dad?" He stared into his father's face. "Is that you?"

Jesse stepped into the cabin. "Colt?"

"What the heck happened to you, Dad?"

"Is that you, boy?" In raced the heelers, wagging their tails.

"How'd you get here, Dad?"

"What are *you* doing up here banging?"

"There's a cougar out there. I thought you were it!"

No point in mentioning that he also thought his dad was the ghost of Jackson Parker—but just for that one minute. "Shut the door, Dad!"

"What door?"

Someone in a poncho was right behind. "You okay, Colt? What's going on?"

"Cheryl?"

She slid back the hood. "What are you doing up here, Colt?"

"I saw a cougar. And a big ol' paw print in the mud. Heard it scream. How'd you two get here so quick?"

Jesse said, "Well, it wasn't all that quick, Colt. Six hours."

"From where?"

"Drove straight through from Winnemucca, except to stop for gas."

"In the Corvette?"

"Pedal to the metal." He nodded in Cheryl's direction. "With her driving. I can't shift with this thing."

"What the heck happened to you this time?"

"The arm is thanks to the Red Volcano. He busted that for me at the Buffalo Bill Cody Stampede Rodeo. Took a surgeon to screw it back together right.

"Then, since I was off the bulls for a while, last week I figured I'd help the boys out a little with the rodeo livestock."

"Out there with his arm in a cast," muttered Cheryl. "What kind of sense does that make?" She reached under her poncho and pulled a Butterfinger bar out of her pocket. "Here, Colt. I brought you this. It might be busted up."

"Yeah, well, a bronc got hung up in the gate and went down, with his front legs caught between the slats. So me and the boys were all up there trying to free his hooves and set him loose, but before it was over he kicked me in the face, and the next thing you know I'm spitting out teeth and blood, but I'm all right."

"What about the bronc?"

"Okay, too."

"Jesse?" said Cheryl. "Call and say we got him and say there's a cougar up here. Let the others know to come on in now."

She dialed and gave Jesse the phone. "Celeste? . . . We got him. He was holed up in a cabin. There's a cougar up here someplace." He listened. "Well, the horses and dogs are quiet, can't be too close by. I know, I know, Celeste . . ." He hung on a minute, waiting. "Okay, yeah." He waited again. "Paramedics? Heck no, nothing wrong with him. He has a candy bar. Just send the cowboys up as soon as they can see what's out there and tell the deputies thanks, we'll take it from here." He listened. "Yeah, that'd be good. You're breaking up, Celeste. Okay. I'll tell him."

He closed the phone. "Soon as it gets light, Angelo and some cowboys are comin' up with rifles. Just in case. The sheriff will call in Fish and Game to come on out later and look around."

"Okay." Colton divided the candy bar into three pieces, but Cheryl and Jesse said no.

"And your ma says you've got some explaining to do."

"Okay."

"You owe me, boy."

"I do?"

"The call wasn't breakin' up. She's mad as a hornet."

"She is?"

No surprise there.

"Better call Wes, too," Cheryl said. "He's just out there worried sick."

"The sheriff was thinkin' that's where you might be headed," Cheryl whispered as she dialed again and handed Jesse the phone.

"It's Jess. Up in a cabin. He saw a cougar. Yeah, me too. Guess it worked. No, I know. Okay then. Get some sleep." He closed the phone. "Grandpa says good boy."

Well, that was nice to hear.

"He's been sitting up all night. Wishin' on every star. Talkin' to the Powers That Be. Okay, then," Jesse said quietly. "Let's build us a fire and warm you up and warm up those pups. That one's about to pop."

He went outside the door and crashed around in the brush and dragged some sticks up against the steps and stomped on them, broke them up.

Colton started with what was left in the stove, added some thin twigs, then small sticks, then small branches—all wet, but that wouldn't matter. One thing Colton knew for sure: the chimney was dented up pretty good, but at least he'd banged it clean.

"You still smoke?" Colton asked him.

"Who wants to know?"

"I need a lighter. There's just one old matchstick left."

"Well, that shouldn't stop you from building a fire, boy." Jesse dug into his jacket pocket and handed Colton a plastic lighter and a folded-up Stampede Rodeo program.

"I thought you said you quit."

Colton balled up the rodeo program, poked it in, and lit the corner with the lighter. Soon, pale light flickered in the room. The heelers snoozed quietly on a moth-eaten rug.

Jesse laughed. "Looks like you busted this place up pretty good, Colt."

"You should talk, Dad."

They pulled up chairs and the stool to watch the flames. "Yeah, so we were on our way to Cheryl's cousin Annie's wedding. Came down out of a canyon—"

"A wedding? Lookin' like that?"

"Came into cell phone range, and the phone rang and it was your mother. Asked if I'd heard from you, and I said, No, why?

"She said you were gone. Said she went out for a while and a neighbor lady stopped by and couldn't find you anywhere. She thought you'd run off someplace."

"Run off? Why would I do that?"

"That's what I said."

Colton shook his head. "So she went and asked Louise to check up on me. I should have figured she'd pull something like that."

"And she said you'd been talking about wanting to live out in Idaho with me or Grandpa, instead of her. Asked about where the train went. Said you hadn't had much of an appetite lately. Now, that did concern me."

"Well, I'm not that big on squash ravioli if that means I lost my appetite."

"Said you seemed distant. Hangin' out in your room. Said you wouldn't go to dinner, even for a rib eye. Is that true?"

"I've rethought that one."

"I bet you have. Said they found a poem you hid that a girl wrote you. Nobody seemed to know who the girl was."

"They looked under my pillow? That's my secret hiding place."

"Boy, that's everybody's secret hiding place in case you didn't know it.

"She said you didn't want to go to a cowboy movie."

"With subtitles?"

"Wanted to quit the soccer team."

"I just said that to rile her up."

"Well, whatever. She said she had an uneasy feeling about leaving you alone. Then the neighbor lady called to ask if you went with her, and she and her friend hurried on back.

"They looked around the ranch, called the sheriff. Then called me.

"All that was missing was you, your hat, your boots, and your Carhartt. And your piggy bank was raided, and the cork was on the floor. They figured you took off. Maybe thought about taking the train or a bus."

"Now why would I do something that stupid? And that piggy money's in an envelope."

"Well, anyway—"

"Under the mattress. For a walking stick for Grandpa, that he won't know is a cane!"

"She said she saw where you checked PRCA on the Internet. Printed out my picture. Is it a good one?"

"Not bad."

"And she called up your teacher. He said you wrote in your journal you couldn't wait to come on back to Idaho. Wanted to go to a rodeo. But he didn't think anything of it."

"Can't wait? That's just an expression."

"Anyway, he called some others to come up and search. We pulled in about two this morning. That's a good neighbor you got there—Angelo. Lent his ponies and the dogs.

"Took about ten minutes to saddle up. The moon was up.

Rode past here . . . they said up here had already been checked."

I knew I heard horses' hooves, Colton thought, but never mind about the ghost rider now.

"We rode way on up, up past a lake, figuring maybe you got hurt up there somehow. There wasn't any sign of you; we backtracked. The fat one kept running ahead. We decided to let her lead."

"Her name is Lily. She's not fat, she's pregnant. A horse ran her over and broke her tail," said Colton.

"Well, I can relate to that." Jesse leaned down and patted her. "You're pretty anyway, tail or not," he told the heeler.

"Did Mom see you?"

"Yeah."

"Was she mad?"

"Yeah."

Cheryl looked down at her engagement ring and fiddled with it. "There's only so many times you can get clobbered in the head, Jesse. She's right."

"You know what, lady? You need to think about your own self. Remember how tricky that trick riding got out in Billings last summer?"

Jesse and Cheryl had a stare-down for a couple of minutes.

Then Jesse said, "How else does she expect me to make a living?"

Cheryl didn't answer.

"I've got one thing on my résumé: Professional Rodeo Cowboys Association."

"You've also got Clean Plate Club, Dad."

"I didn't go to college like Celeste did. I don't have a rich uncle to give me a ranch."

"It wasn't college. It was culinary school. The Hudsons already have a ranch!"

"And when Celeste and me split, that rich great-uncle of hers wrote me a letter and told me"—he glanced at Cheryl—"well, I won't say it in the presence of a lady."

"What was it, Dad?"

Jesse whispered to Colton.

"Whoa! Frank wrote that?"

"Yeah, and I wish he could find something good to say about me sometime. And I wish your ma would, too!"

"She says you're fearless."

"Not anymore I'm not." Colton's dad looked at the floor. "I just got scared witless. My whole world got rocked.

"Scared to death you might have got drug off someplace. Or were laying hurt and bloody somewhere, out in the dark and alone. Saw that big black lake up there. Wondered if . . .

"I said to Whoever Might Be Listening, just give me some kind of signal, some kind of sign. Just something to go on."

He stopped talking for a moment.

"Right then, I saw one puff of smoke rise up from below. Just one. Caught the moonlight. Then it disappeared.

"So we rode on down. Anyway . . ." He lifted his good arm and wiped his eyes with his sleeve.

"It's okay, Jess," Cheryl said gently. "Everything's okay now."

Colton said, "I built a fire in the stove but thought better of it. Thought maybe the chimney needed cleaning."

Jesse walked to the doorway, leaned down, pressed his cast against one nostril, and blew his nose into the dark.

"My word, Jesse, I wish you wouldn't do that," Cheryl told him.

"Sorry. I thought I learned that from you."

"You did not."

"I was scarin' away the cougar."

"No you weren't."

"Frank has an old donkey engine out there in the pump house," Colton said. "One cylinder."

"Does it run?"

"No."

"You two stay where you are," Cheryl told them.

"There's a black widow spider behind it."

"Stay here, I mean it," Cheryl told him.

"Yes, ma'am."

"Two words I suggest you learn from the get-go, Colton. If I had a ma," he added, "then maybe I'd've learned 'Yes, ma'am' quicker."

"And learned to use a handkerchief," added Cheryl. "But it's never too late, Jesse."

They sat and watched the fire.

Colton got up and looked out the doorway. Everything was silver, black, and wet. The Appaloosas were grazing a few feet away—white spots bright in the moonlight. Leaves on the old fruit trees were shiny; some had fallen to the ground. Wispy clouds covered and uncovered the moon. Jesse called, "Hey, Colt."

"What?"

"Who's Maddie?"

Colton answered: "You still scared of spiders, Dad?"

Eleven

Colton heard sticks cracking and voices coming closer. Angelo rode up out of the trees with Enrique and his uncle Alberto wearing white cowboy hats and carrying rifles in saddle scabbards.

Angelo called, "Hey, Colt."

"Hey."

Enrique said, "Manuel's down at the house."

He was?

Colton and his dad broke the fire up and shut down the stove.

Then Jesse untied an Appaloosa. He pulled Colton up behind him with his good arm. Colton glanced over his shoulder at the cabin, with the door broken. A eucalyptus branch was lying on the roof. A flock of wild turkeys was sitting on a limb above it.

Cheryl got up on the other horse, and they all headed down.

It was quiet, except for the sounds of the horses' hooves and the frogs singing, until two peacocks strutted out of the trees. One let out a scream.

"What the heck's she yellin' about?" Colton's dad asked him.

Colton could see Celeste coming. "Why did you wander off?" she called.

"It's a he, Dad."

"Because he's a twelve-year-old kid," Jesse told her. "Who lost a cat."

Celeste fired back: "I know how old my son is! I know he lost a cat, Jesse! I actually live with this boy in case you haven't noticed."

"Whoa now," said Jesse. "Calm down, girl."

"Don't you tell me to calm down!"

"Darlin'?" said Jesse. "I'm talkin' to the horse."

"Good luck, boy," his dad whispered as they both slid off.

Angelo and the others went ahead—rode the horses through the gate and led them into the barn.

Celeste stood staring at Colton. "I asked you a question."

"I heard a meow," Colton told her.

"Do you know what was about to happen? When I got the call saying you were okay?"

"No, ma'am."

"The sheriff was just about to start a helicopter search. Do you know there were people all up and down the road looking for you?"

"Yes, ma'am."

"Do you know that my eighty-six-year-old great-uncle Frank has been up all night? That he's called me every hour?"

"No, ma'am."

"Don't no ma'am, yes ma'am me! I know that trick!" She shot a glance at Colton's dad. "He could have died up there last night I hope you know."

"Yeah, well, he didn't. Colt hung tight, just like he's supposed to do."

Her cell phone rang. Celeste reached into her pocket. "This is probably Frank again. Yes, Frank, they're down. Sure . . ." She handed the phone to Colton. "He wants to know more about the cougar."

After Colton gave the report to Frank, Celeste took back the phone and told Colton, "This still smells like fish and chips, I hope you know."

"Don't ask," Colton told his dad.

"Your son stashed fish and chips in my purse."

"It was only the fish."

Colton leaned closer to his dad and whispered, "It was for Smoke. From the Sea Foam."

"It was? In Reno?"

Celeste didn't answer.

"You still got that dealer's outfit?"

"No!"

Celeste looked for a long moment at Colton and his dad, standing in matching jackets, boots, and hats.

She shook her head.

Colton decided to test the water. "Mom?"

"What?"

"Blackjack."

He thought he saw the beginning of a smile.

"See you down at the house," she told them.

"Flapjacks!" Colton called.

Jesse called, "Me and Cheryl can make a run for some bacon!"

"Angelo has homemade sausages!" she hollered back.

"Now yer talkin', lady!"

Colton walked a little behind his mom, to give her some space to cool off.

Just then Louise came up the driveway. "You were up in that darn cabin all night?" she whispered. "I checked that cabin first thing. It was all locked up. I didn't hear a sound." She raised her palms in the air. "Checked the door. Called 'Co-o-o-o-o-o-o-lton! Co-o-o-o-o-lt' as loud as I could. I'm sorry, Jesse. I lost my voice!"

Hmmm. That raspy whisper. And rattly door. It was *Louise*?

"I stopped by with some cookies for you, Colton—and you were gone!"

"Did you look in the old pump house, too? With the squeaky hinge?"

"Yes. Why do you ask?"

"Just wondering." No point in saying he'd thought she was the ghost of Jackson Parker.

Jesse gave Louise a hug. "Don't worry, darlin'. It all worked out fine."

He paused.

"Where are the cookies?"

"Down in the hutch."

"What kind?"

"Banana oatmeal with carob chips."

"Well, I'll eat anything."

Next came Dino and Mr. Viramontes. And Elmo—running, for once. Jesse shook hands with everybody. "Thanks again. See you down at the house." He went on over to the barn to help the others pull the saddles off and brush the horses down.

"Well, I guess you got more information than you expected for that puma report," Mr. Viramontes said. He gave Colton a big squeeze around his shoulders, and Colton looked at the ground.

He noticed Elmo's big, round, wide footprints in the mud.

"Well, it may not have been one," Colton said.

"Did your gut tell you that was a cougar?" Dino asked.

"Yeah."

Colton looked down at Elmo, strolling beside him. That lazy boy would never go all the way up to the spring. Would he?

"Okay then," said Dino. "Bet you it was."

But my gut told me Louise was a cougar, too, thought Colton.

And a ghost.

"In any event, you did the right thing."

"Yes, you certainly did," said Mr. Viramontes. "No question of that, Colton. Good job."

Dino lowered his voice. "Give your mother a day or two to simmer down. She's just upset."

There weren't any patrol cars parked in the driveway. Good. Not that Colton didn't respect police officers, he did. And appreciate what they did, or were trying to do. He was embarrassed, that's all. So he was relieved to see it was just Manuel standing on the porch waiting for him, and nobody else. "How big was the puma?"

"Big. If it was one."

"They thought you took off, man. We knew you didn't, though. We knew you were out there somewhere. I wanted to help search for you, but they said no kids. You had me scared, though," Manuel told Colton. "I thought maybe somebody grabbed you."

Two officers from Fish and Game drove up the driveway in a green truck with a gun rack in the back window. They talked to Colton for a few minutes and told everyone to stay close to home. They gave out some pamphlets. Then they headed up the two ruts that led to the upper lake and the canyon beyond.

Colton and Manuel took the soccer ball out to the field on the side of the house. Elmo and Lily tagged along, and

Elmo sat in the middle of the field, relaxing. Manuel's dad, Uncle Alberto, Mr. Viramontes, and Dino couldn't resist joining in. They played around awhile; then it heated up. Manuel passed to his dad, who dribbled the ball around Elmo and passed it to Dino, who booted it past Uncle Alberto—down to the fence. Mr. Viramontes was fast! He dove for it.

Goal!

Lily jumped on him and licked his nose.

Alberto gave him a hand up. They were both laughing. And Colton thought, Yeah, Jared was right.

A puppy would be right up Mr. Viramontes's alley. Right along with coaching a team.

Heelers were good dogs, they were! Especially Lily's pups would be. He'd get Jared to work on their teacher till he caved in. Jared wasn't a bad kid, really—and he was smart, had good advice. Just needed to develop some horse sense.

Everybody said thanks and congratulated one another and all that—shook hands with Jesse, Cheryl, and Celeste. And Colton. And one another. Everybody was happy and re-lieved. Colton's family was grateful—people knew that. They invited everybody for breakfast but no one stayed. Too beat.

Dino and Mr. Viramontes were the last two in the drive-way. Dino extended his hand. "George? Great to connect again. Been too long. Thanks again for calling everybody, bringing us all up here. Happy ending—love that."

"Yeah, I'll say."

"Think about coaching next year," Dino told him. "And let's see if we can get Enrique and Alberto involved. Those guys. Wow."

Mr. Viramontes said, "I know what you mean."

Great! Now Dino was working on him!

Inside, Angelo fixed breakfast—pancakes, scrambled eggs, homemade sausages, coffee, and biscuits. Frank showed up, and everybody ate, then sat around while the sun rose higher in the sky.

Colton was outside with his dad and Angelo checking out the Jag when the Fish and Game officers returned.

They watched the truck bump down the road, then park. The officers got out and looked into the bed of the pickup.

"Well, they got something back there," said Jesse.

Colton had a sick feeling in his heart, imagining the lifeless body of a big cat lying in the truck bed—mouth open a little, pink tongue hanging out between its fangs. And dripping blood and saliva out the side of its mouth. Sure he was scared of the cougar, but he didn't want it to die!

Jesse and Angelo walked over together. Colton couldn't go closer. He could hear the conversation. "The only cat up there was one dead kitty cat, by a pile of brush," one of the officers told them. "Not sure what got it."

The officer lifted the tarp, and Colton's dad and Angelo looked under. "Came upon it in the field, just layin' there. Big guy. Eyes open, like yellow glass marbles."

"Colt? You want to come here and take a look?"

Colton couldn't. He felt like he'd gotten kicked in the

chest. "No." Something got Smoke—just like Colton had been afraid had happened.

"No sign of a cougar, though," the officer was saying. "Nothing. No prints by the spring or anywhere else; the rain's washed everything away up there. The fire in the backcountry could have forced a cougar out.

"Anyway, the rain's cooled everything down. Maybe it headed home. It's hard to judge animals from a distance, though. Could have been a bobcat. Coyote. A dog, even. We'll continue to investigate."

His dad turned his back; Colton couldn't hear what they were talking about anymore. He didn't want to hear.

The officers got into the truck and drove away, but Colton's dad stood in the driveway, quietly talking with Angelo.

Then his dad came up to Colton, alone. Colton looked at the ground.

"It was Smoke under there, wasn't it, Dad?"

"No, son. It was a big ol' half-dead barn owl. They'll take it down to see if something can be done for it. It wasn't in very good shape. Sad to see it . . . Looked scared to death. Said if they can patch it up, they'll bring it on back here. Release it. So, you never know."

He paused.

"There was a dead cat they saw up there, though."

"Oh."

His dad rested his cast on Colton's shoulder. "I asked what

color, and they said it had spots. So it wasn't Smoke. Hang in there, son. Don't give up on him yet. You never know about a cat. Just when you least expect it, he might walk right through that door."

"Okay." Don't lose it, Colton told himself.

He looked sideways at the cast, at his dad's huge fingers and thumb sticking out of the end. "Sorry you and Cheryl came all the way out for nothing."

"For nothing? Not hardly."

Colton looked closer at the back of his dad's hand. Part of a bull's-head tattoo was showing, just above his knuckles. "When'd you get the tattoo?"

"Never go directly from a bar to a tattoo parlor, son."

"I won't, Dad."

"Okay then. We better git."

Already? Colton wished his dad would stay. And Cheryl.

"Take care, Colt."

"You too, Dad."

"Don't poke any rattlesnakes."

"I won't. You either."

"Don't try to get taller than me."

"Yeah, just wait."

"Angelo? Thanks, man."

"Sure you two don't want to stay?" Angelo asked.

"Can't, but thanks," said Colton's dad.

"Angelo has a bunkhouse," Celeste told Cheryl. "You've been up all night."

"I'll pull in someplace after a while. We should try to make it partway back to Winnemucca. To my cousin's reception—if we can."

"Well, come on back," said Angelo. "The door's always open. We'll fish up at the lake. There's some big sturgeon up there. Thirty pounds."

Jesse said, "Maybe we'll take you up on that. And likewise, come on out our way. Colton pulled a six-pound brown out of the South Fork last July."

Angelo asked Colton, "What'd you get it on?"

Colton told him: "Royal Coachman Wulff."

"I'm going to beat that next July," Jesse announced.

Colton said, "Don't count on it."

"Take care, Jesse," Celeste said. "And, Jesse? This time tell the dentist, not so white on the new teeth. Nice to meet you, Cheryl. After all this time."

"Likewise."

Cheryl put down the top and opened the driver's side door of the Corvette. "See ya, Colt."

She crossed her fingers and held them up. "For Smoke."

Colton wanted to give Cheryl a hug.

Just do it! he told himself.

Well, next time.

His dad called him over. "Open up the glove box," he said.

Colton pushed the silver button on the glove compartment, and the door fell open.

"Take it, Colt. It's yours."

He saw his dad's championship buckle, with the belt coiled around it like a snake.

Colton was quiet. "You sure?"

"Sure I'm sure."

"Thanks, Dad." He paused. "How will you hold your pants up?"

"That's my problem, boy."

Twelve

At school on Monday, Mr. Viramontes asked Colton if he cared to share what happened, and Colton didn't really, but he agreed to anyway. He kept it short.

"Now you tell," Mr. Viramontes told Manuel. "From your perspective."

Manuel told about his dad getting the call from Mr. Viramontes and them going up to Colton's with Uncle Alberto and about the police asking him questions, about if he thought Colton ran away and how he said no.

He told about everybody pairing off and looking in different directions and then about Colton's dad showing up in the middle of the night.

He talked about playing Pictionary with Ms. Jensen and the others while they waited for the sun to come up far enough to bring Colton down from the mountain.

And then how fun it was, everybody playing soccer for a little while and about how Lily licked Mr. Viramontes's nose.

Jared raised his hand. "Colton. Don't you think it's time to get another cat? And stop looking for your old cat in the middle of the night? I do! People could have gotten hurt out there in the dark looking for you! Ever think of that, Colton? Huh?"

"Jared," said Mr. Viramontes. "You've got lots of opinions for us as usual." He paused. "But Jared raises some interesting questions. So let me ask you, Colton: Was there something you'd have done differently?"

Sure there was.

"I'd have to think about that."

"Anything else you want to share?"

Maybe so. Colton took the horseback photo of him and his dad on Sugar and the Yellowstone photo out of his math book and pinned them to the wall. Why shouldn't they be in his Student of the Month display?

National Bull Riding Champion—two years in a row: now, that had to say something. No matter what his mom said or thought about the rodeo: Colton was proud of his dad, always had been and always would be. Sure, he hoped his dad would quit bull riding, but if he didn't, that was his decision. Nobody could make it for him. The rodeo was his life. Colton knew that.

"Who's the cowboy?" Jared asked.

"My dad."

He could have said he was a legend. He could have said he had a buckle at home to match the one his dad was wearing in the picture.

Jared looked at the photos for a long time. For once, he kept his mouth shut and didn't ask any questions.

Later, when his mom picked him up from practice, Colton asked, "Mom? What happened to that picture of you and dad, with you in your Golden Bounty casino girl getup?"

"Why do you ask?"

"I like that picture. You took it out of the album."

"So what?"

"Did you throw it out?"

"No."

"Good."

"How did soccer go?"

"Great. I stunk, but it was fun."

Soccer was always upbeat. Dino made sure of that. He was a great coach—the best.

Colton wasn't sleeping with any soccer balls yet, but it wasn't outside the range of possibility. He looked forward to moving from the pretty bad range into the okay range sometime soon. With Dino behind him, he'd get there.

The hillsides were golden; sunlight shimmered in the trees.

"I have a surprise for you," Colton's mom told him.

"Is it Smoke?"

"I would tell you if it was Smoke."

"What is it then?"

"You'll see."

"Mom?" Colton said. "If it's another cat, I don't want it."

They drove up the driveway, parked, and went inside.

Colton folded his arms on his chest and watched his mother unlatch the metal grid of the Pet Taxi. "Remember when you said you thought you heard a meow?"

Celeste reached way into the back of the carrier. "Look what Angelo saw run out from under the old brush pile near the windmill. And back in again."

She stood up, holding a kitten. "Have you ever seen markings like this?" The kitten flattened her ears and hissed at Colton. "She's feral—born in the wild. Angelo caught her by throwing his hat over her. Isn't that silly?"

Colton said nothing.

"And he took off his shirt and wrapped her in it. And carried her home with her head poking out. She growled and complained the whole way. But she alternates between growling, hissing, and purring like a motorboat, and she doesn't scratch or bite. So far. I think she's just scared."

"What if she's somebody's?"

"Way out here? No way." Celeste was quiet for a moment. "The dead cat up there, that the Fish and Game people saw, Angelo went up and found her, and buried her. Similar markings as this—looked like part Bengal. Bengals are exotic cats, part Asian Leopard cat—and a little on the wild side."

Colton gazed out the window.

"Angelo thinks it was the kitten's mom. Look, Colt—so tiny . . . Angelo said the minute he saw her, he wondered if you'd take her in and give her a home."

Colton looked past the mountain. The sun had sunk beneath the horizon. It was growing dark. A moth fluttered against the windowpane.

"Then later he thought he'd better check the brush pile again to make sure another one wasn't around, and out crept another one. Meowing his head off. Hungry. A boy. That looks just like this one. He had the vet look them both over; they got their first set of shots. And worm pills. They're healthy—just need some TLC. Oh, calm down," Colton's mother told the kitten.

"The brother's wilder. Angelo will look for a home for him—once he tames him a little bit. Unless you want to take him, too."

"I don't even want this one!"

The kitten began to purr. Colton felt guilty, saying that in front of a little lost kitten. But it was true!

"Smoke hasn't been gone much more than a week. I don't want a replacement, Mom."

"The vet says that's a nervous purr, but it sounds like a regular old purr to me."

All was quiet except for the kitten purring.

"She's not a replacement. She's herself—a little lost kitty who needs a home. Nobody says we're giving up on Smoke."

Yeah, right.

"The vet says that feral kittens can make wonderful pets—but only if you bond with them young enough. Colton? Lookee here. Have you ever seen spots like this?"

Colton looked at the black splotches on the kitten's belly. "Angelo think it's the Bengal in her that gives her the glittery coat. See how glittery she is?"

Colton didn't care about glittery.

Celeste held the kitten up close to the light. "Apricot fur. Black spots. What a combo! And check out those peeps."

Colton looked at the floor.

"Eyes like a sunrise. Angelo calls her Lucia. It's Italian for 'light.' But we can call her whatever we want."

Colton didn't want to call her anything. He ate dinner in silence, washed the dishes, then went upstairs to his room and closed his door. He got into his pajamas and looked at a magazine.

When he heard his mom coming up the steps, he quickly got under the covers. He reached over and turned off the light switch.

She opened the door. "I know you're awake," she whispered. She put the kitten on his bed, but the kitten hissed and scrambled off and under it.

"Grandma Lucy's name also means 'light.' "

"Well, call her Lucy then. She's not Italian."

"Fine. I'll get the litter box."

"Oh great," said Colton.

He pretended to sleep.

Celeste came back up with a plastic pan full of Kitty Litter. She shoved it under his bed. "Here. Learn how to use this," she told the kitten.

Colton heard a long, low growl.

Celeste plopped down on the edge of his mattress. "Colton?"

"What?"

"All of us—me, Dad, Cheryl, Angelo, Grandpa. Frank. Everybody—we want what's best for you."

"I know."

"As long as you understand that."

"I do."

"Your dad and I talked on the phone for a long while today. We resolved to try to pull it together as a family more. See more of each other. He's talking about quitting the bulls."

We'll see, Colton said to himself.

"The rodeo is all he's ever known. He wants me to be more open to it; I said I'd work on that."

"Can we all meet at the rodeo in Reno sometime?"

"Maybe. We'll see what the future brings. Maybe Idaho is in the cards for you. We'll talk about it down the road. Who knows? Maybe ranching school. But for now, you're stuck with me."

"I am?"

"Yes."

"Well, that stinks."

She bopped him with a pillow.

"Ow! Only kidding!" It didn't really hurt.

"Love you, Ma."

And Colton did love Celeste—although it had been a while since he'd said it. Or called her Ma.

"Love you, Colt."

It was a while since she'd called him Colt, too.

Colton snuggled up under the covers. He heard the kitten purring, like a faraway motorboat.

Would he really want to leave and go back to Idaho? Colton didn't know. He didn't have to know—not now, anyway. It wasn't his call. In the future, they could talk about it. That's what counted most.

He closed his eyes.

For now, all was good.

Except for Smoke.

He woke at dawn. Pale light filled his room. He leaned on one elbow and looked out the window behind the bookshelf. The boulders and oaks on the hill behind the barn made black spots and splotches against the apricot sky.

Venus was shining, bright and clear. Above the barn, the moon was a fingernail slit in the sky with light leaking through it.

Below the moon and the star, on the peak of the barn roof, Colton saw a black silhouette of an owl.

It flew.

He thought of the barn owl in the back of the Fish and Game truck.

Alone. In the dark. Under a tarp. Had he made it?

Maybe not.

Colton thought of Smoke disappearing into the night. What a great kitty Smoke was. He hoped somebody found him and took him in. And he hoped whoever found him would look for ads in the paper and check the Internet and bring him home.

But he knew it was more likely that Smoke had died, somehow. Like Lucy's mom, maybe. Maybe whatever got her, got him.

Or maybe he'd been carried off by a coyote—a coyote that came in close, and hungry—because of the fire in the backcountry. Or a bobcat.

Or maybe it was the cougar.

Colton didn't believe the cougar was a coyote or a dog. Only one thing moved like a cougar: a cougar.

Like Dino said: Colton should trust his gut feelings on that.

Colton knew his mom was right: For every happy ending, there was a heartbreaker. There was a Luke.

And maybe a Smoke.

Colton blinked, and big tears slid down his face, but so what? You could cry about a pet and still be a man. He'd learned that from Mr. Viramontes. Louise said Mr. Viramontes was a medic in Vietnam. You couldn't get any braver than that.

Colton just let the tears fall and didn't try to stop them.

Why should he? He'd lost Smoke, and he loved Smoke. And Smoke loved him back. Smoke was one of the best friends he'd ever had.

Maybe he was sunlight in the trees, like Frank said. Maybe he was in heaven, playing with Luke. Smoke didn't mind big ol' doggies. He liked them!

Sure Colton knew about caterpillars and butterflies and eggs and owls and all that, but he didn't know any more about heaven than his grandpa did, or if cats or dogs got to go. But even if Smoke just went back into the earth, turned to dust—was dust on a rock rolling in space—that was all right, too. He was a miracle, like everything else.

Colton had figured that out sitting with his grandpa the night the stars shot and fell, and the moon rose into the sky.

Colton could see a pattern of light and shadows moving on the wall across the room. He knew that the sun was rising and the wind was stirring the leaves of the tree outside the window behind him.

Lucy clawed her way up the side of the bed. She sat on Colton's pillow and yawned.

Colton carried her to the window. He showed her the barn and the rocky hill behind it. He carried her to the other side of the room and moved the curtain aside so they could look in the opposite direction. They could see the driveway leading to the road—and to the east, rows of olive trees, and above them, the canyon that wound between grassy hills to the horizon. Maybe he'd ride the Appaloosas up into that canyon with Angelo and Celeste.

Maybe Manuel and his dad and uncle could ride along.

It was nice of Angelo to go up and bury Lucy's mama. And bring Lucy in from the brush pile. Or Lucia—or whatever her name was going to be. And bring her brother in, too. How would you like to be a baby kitten alone in the world, with no mama? Or daddy.

Colton's dad was right: Angelo was a very good guy. He wasn't a know-it-all. He knew a lot. Could back it up. He was a hard worker and a volunteer firefighter. He had a good heart. And Angelo was a good match for his mom. Anyone could see that.

Maybe Colton would invite him to the next scrimmage. When was it? He checked the schedule.

He heard the sounds of tires on gravel. And an engine idling. Probably Angelo—up with the chickens. Working on his truck; lately it had been running rough. Maybe Colton would take a walk over and see what was going on. Give him a hand.

Colton put Lucy down on the rug. "You stay here," he told her, and she darted under his bed. Colton got dressed, put on his boots and hat, and thumped down the stairs. He stood outside Celeste's bedroom door and knocked softly. "Mom? I'm going over to Angelo's."

"Now?"

"Yeah, I'll be back. Shall I leave a note?"

"That's not funny, Colton."

He looked out the kitchen window at the plum tree, back-lit with yellow. The hills were hazy purple; above them the sky was tinted pink. He opened the door.

Madison?

What was she doing there!

In a bathrobe and slippers shaped like ducks?

"Listen up! My dad just called from Boston. He and Gavin got there, and when they opened up the back of the rental truck, a big black cat jumped out. Big, meaning huge."

Colton stared at her.

"One white whisker. Yellow eyes. Big as a raccoon. He's at my brother's apartment, making him sneeze. And my mom needs to talk to your mom. We don't have your telephone number."

Celeste came out of her bedroom, wearing a pink flannel nightgown with hearts all over it. Now where'd she get that?

"Is everything okay?" she asked.

"Hi! I'm Madison."

"Ah! So *you're* Madison."

"Smoke's in Boston, Mom!" Colton told her.

"Nice to meet you, Madison. I'm Celeste." Her eyes widened. *"What?"*

"He rode all the way to Boston with my dad and my brother in the back of a moving truck," Madison said. "My dad took him to a pet clinic, and they hydrated him. They said he's fine. My dad's bringing him back on the plane in a couple of days."

"You. Must. Be. Kidding," said Celeste.

"We're so sorry."

"Don't apologize! Hey, that boy loves trucks! I'm sure he enjoyed the ride completely."

Celeste waved to Madison's mom, sitting in the pickup truck—and walked across the gravel in her bare feet to say hello.

Colton stood there, looking at Madison. And Madison stood there, looking back. "I told you, Colt."

"Yeah, I know."

Talk about the long way home!

The sun was rising behind Kingston Mountain. A jet drew a golden line across the sky.

Smoke was flying from Boston to California?

Who would have thought it! Colton couldn't even have dreamed up an ending better than that.

Except maybe . . .

"Stay right there," he told Madison. Colton ran upstairs. Lucy was sitting on the windowsill. Colton picked her up and carried her downstairs. He held her up for Madison to see. "What do you think about this little kitty cat?" Lucy hissed and left her mouth open a little, as a threat. There was a black line around her lips. Like a cougar.

"I think she's beautiful!"

"You do? Well, she has a twin who needs a home. Same polka dots and everything. Except he's a boy."

"Purrrrrfect!" Madison took Lucy from Colton. "I'll ask."

Celeste and Madison's mom were standing beside the truck, talking and laughing. Madison ran over and gave the kitten to her mom. "I want the boy just like this. Could I, Mom? Please, Mom. At least think about it."

She turned around and walked back over and said, "So, Colt. Let me try on that hat."

Colton handed Madison the hat, and she put it on. She kicked off her slippers. "And the boots."

Yes, ma'am, Colton said to himself.

Madison waited for him to take off his boots.

"My mom has a white silk cowgirl shirt that I can borrow. That my dad bought her in Scottsdale, Arizona. On their honeymoon. With arrows on the pockets. And horses on the front, rearing up."

Colton stood there in his socks as Madison pulled on his boots.

Colton figured she must have been six feet tall in that hat and those boots.

"So, for the dance, all I would need is a cowgirl skirt. After my mom finishes the black cat with the light-up eyes, and the ghost cookies, she can sew me one. With white fringe."

Madison—as a cowgirl?

Nice!

She stood with one fist on her hip.

Then she pushed the hat back farther on her head and smiled. "How do I look?"

Well, the hat was too big and the brim was bent. And the boots were too big . . .

"Sweet."

Colton looked at the ground.

Whoa.

Did he just say that out loud?